A secret room . . .

Eleanor looked doubtfully up into the darkness at the top. "It's probably just more old trunks up there," she said.

"Probably," said Edward. He looked up, too.

"You go first," said Eleanor, looking at him.

Edward paused, then put his foot on the bottom step. "All right," he said. He climbed sturdily upward.

"Well?" she said.

"I can't see," said Edward. "There, now I'm getting used to it. There's the window. There's . . ." His voice stopped. He stood stock-still.

"Tell me!" demanded Eleanor.

"Oh—" said Edward. His voice caught.

THE HALL FAMILY CHRONICLES

◆

THE HALL FAMILY CHRONICLES

The
Diamond
in the
Window

JANE LANGTON

■ HarperTrophy®

An Imprint of HarperCollins*Publishers*

Library of Congress Catalog Card Number: 62-7312
ISBN 0-06-440042-5 (pbk.) 12/06 3455 4062

Typography by Larissa Lawrynenko
❖
First Harper Trophy edition, 1973
Visit us on the World Wide Web!
www.harperchildrens.com

For Christopher and David

On him the light of star and moon
Shall fall with purer radiance down . . .
Him Nature giveth for defense
His formidable innocence;
The mounting sap, the shells, the sea,
All spheres, all stones, his helpers be . . .

—RALPH WALDO EMERSON

Contents

The
Diamond
in the
Window

I

EDWARD MISBEHAVES

EDWARD HALL SAT UNDER the front porch of the big house on Walden Street in Concord, Massachusetts, and thought about his two ambitions in life. The first was to be the President of the United States. That was not very likely, but it was at least possible. The second was unlikely and impossible altogether, because he had been born into the wrong family. Why, oh, why wasn't his name "Robert Robinson" instead of "Edward Hall"?

Eddy took out of his pocket a collection of bottle caps, matchboxes, and pennies and arranged them on the ground in a decorative pattern. If only fathers and mothers would be more careful when they chose names for their children! If only they would pick names that sounded well in Backwards English! "Edward Hall," for example, was all right in ordinary English, but it was terrible the other way around—"Drawde Llah" didn't sound like anything. But "Robert Robinson"—there was a name! If you turned it backwards and softened the "s," it was transformed into a name as strange and fantastic as that of an ambassador from some foreign land—*"Trebor Nosnibor"!* Edward put his two ambitions in life together and whispered under his breath, "Introducing the President of the United States, Mr. Trebor Nosnibor!" How glorious! Edward sighed.

His older sister squeezed through the broken place in the lattice and squatted down beside him. Eleanor was taller and thinner than Edward, and she wore glasses because her eyes were weak. Her hair was red, like his, and it hung in a long pigtail down the middle of her back. Eleanor was very fond of a boy in her class named Benjamin Parks. She switched her long pigtail over her shoulder and stared earnestly through the broken slats. "Someone's coming," she said, "and you know who it is? It's Mr. Preek! What do you suppose he wants with Aunt Lily?"

Mr. Preek was the president of the bank and a selectman. With him was his secretary, Miss Prawn. These two sterling citizens of Concord had decided to take matters into their own hands. In their opinion this affair of the Halls had been allowed to slide along (in the most slipshod way) for far too many years. It was high time some responsible persons did something about it. They meant to, and here they were.

Their faces were grim. Mr. Preek wore a large grim vest. Miss Prawn was swathed about in a grim black cape, although it was a nice warm day in June. She poked her foot at a stove-in place in the porch floor and pursed up her lips.

Aunt Lily came to the door. Her face went white when she saw who her visitors were. "Come in," she said.

The visitors stayed exactly ten minutes. When they came out, Eleanor and Edward were still under the porch, listening through the hole in the floor.

"As soon as I possibly can," said Aunt Lily.

"Seven hundred and twelve dollars is a great deal of money in back taxes, Miss Hall," said Miss Prawn.

"This property would bring a great deal more if you sold it for the price of the land," said Mr. Preek.

"But our house is on it," said Aunt Lily.

"Tear it down and live somewhere else," said Mr. Preek. "Good day, Miss Hall."

Edward and Eleanor listened. They could hear the thump-thump of Mr. Preek's feet, going down the steps, and the crack-crack of Miss Prawn's. Aunt Lily shut the door so quietly it made no noise at all.

Mr. Preek stopped at the gate and looked back. Miss Prawn looked back, too, and shook her head. They were talking about the house. Eleanor and Edward, hidden under the porch, listened with all their ears.

"A monstrosity, of course," Mr. Preek was saying. "Those dreadful towers, those turrets."

"And on such holy ground," said Miss Prawn, "the sacred soil of Concord, cradle of American liberty."

"Where the Minutemen fought the first battle of the American Revolution," said Mr. Preek, "on the nineteenth of April in 1775 at the Old North Bridge!"

"As the crow flies," said Miss Prawn, flapping her black cloak and looking like a crow herself, "hardly a mile from this spot!"

"And do you realize, Miss Prawn," said Mr. Preek, "that this ghastly object is within full view of the home of Ralph Waldo Emerson?" He gazed sadly across the field at the stream of tourists going and coming from Emerson's square white house. "What must they think?" he said.

"And of course," said Miss Prawn, "it's scarcely a quarter of a mile from Orchard House, home of Louisa May Alcott, don't forget that!"

"How could I?" said Mr. Preek. "How could I forget

the author of *Little Women*?"

"And let me remind you, too, Mr. Preek, that this house stands on the very street that leads to Walden Pond, Henry Thoreau's Walden Pond. Did I ever tell you?" said Miss Prawn. "My own dear grandfather put Henry Thoreau in jail!"

"No!" said Mr. Preek. "You never told me! What a glorious heritage!" His brow darkened and he shook his fist at the Halls' big house. "This blot, this stain must come down!"

"Those Halls haven't a leg to stand on, legally," said Miss Prawn.

Mr. Preek looked smug. "No, indeed," he said. "Within the year we'll have it for unpaid taxes, and then—"

(Eleanor and Edward, listening under the porch, stiffened. "Then *what*?" whispered Eddy fiercely.)

Mr. Preek was smiling nastily. He made a gesture like someone striking a match. He held out the hand with the invisible match in the direction of the house. Miss Prawn clapped her hands. "Out in the street they'll be, the four of them!" said Mr. Preek.

This was too much for Edward. He shot through the broken lattice and planted himself in front of Mr. Preek and Miss Prawn. "SUMATOPOPPIH!" cried Edward. (Mr. Preek was quite stout.)

"No, no!" shouted Eleanor, still under the porch on hands and knees.

Miss Prawn and Mr. Preek recoiled from small dirty Eddy and then brushed past him. "Stark raving mad, the lot of them!" said Miss Prawn loudly. "*Everybody* knows it."

"KCITSMOORB!" shouted Edward. (Miss Prawn was rather thin.) Miss Prawn and Mr. Preek looked a little frightened. They scuttled on down the street without looking back.

Eleanor was giggling hysterically. "Oh, Eddy," she said, "you shouldn't have."

2

THE HIDDEN CHAMBER

"WHAT'S THE MATTER with our house?" said Edward. He stood with Eleanor on the bank of the little Mill Brook that ran through the field behind the Emerson place. They were looking back at the house they had grown up in as if they were seeing it for the first time.

"I think it's pretty," said Eleanor. "Of course, it does need painting."

"Yes, it certainly does," said Edward.

"Don't you think it looks a little like the Taj Mahal?" said Eleanor.

All of the other houses on the street were neat square white buildings with dark shutters and simple pitched roofs. Out from among them mushroomed the Halls' house like an exotic tropical plant in a field of New England daisies. It was a great wooden Gothico-Byzantine structure, truly in need of painting. Big as it was, it looked airy and light, as though the wind might pick it up and carry it away. Screened porches ballooned and billowed out of it all around, and domes and towers puffed up at the top as though they were filled with air.

"That's funny," said Edward. "You see that window in the tower, shaped like a keyhole? I don't remember ever looking out of that window, do you?"

Eleanor looked at it. "No," she said, "and it's made of colored glass, too. I'm sure I'd remember looking out of it, if I ever had."

"Come on," said Edward, "let's find it."

At their front gate Eleanor paused. "If Louisa May Alcott or somebody famous like that had lived here once, then they wouldn't talk about burning it down."

"No," said Edward, "they'd charge admission and show you around."

Eleanor looked down hopefully at her little brother. "If only you were already President of the United States, then everybody would want to come and see the house where you were born, and they would pay for it, too."

"By the time I get to be President," said Edward,

"there'll be nothing left of it but ashes."

Eleanor looked up sadly at the house. Then she started talking rapidly in a queer high voice. "Ladies and gentlemen," she said, "if you will kindly line up I will conduct you on a most interesting tour of the birthplace of our great President, Edward P. Hall. Sign the guest book, please."

Edward solemnly pretended to sign. "That will be fifty cents, in advance," quavered Eleanor. "Thank you. Now then, no shoving, right this way. Here before you on the lawn you see the beautiful gazing globe in which our great President used to look as a boy to predict his own glorious future."

Edward peered deep into the shining silver surface of the gazing globe. He pretended to see his future in it and staggered back as if he couldn't believe his eyes. "No!" he said.

Eleanor grabbed his arm and hurried him along. "Now, ladies and gentlemen," she said, "if you will climb the steps and enter the front door (hurry up, Eddy) you will see before you the magnificent insides of our great President's front hall!"

Aunt Lily was in the front hall, sitting at her desk. Her little gooseneck lamp made a tiny spot of light in the gloomy shadows under the vast overarching balcony. Eleanor introduced Aunt Lily to her crowd of invisible tourists. "Here," she said, waving grandly, "you see before you the aged aunt of our great President—Miss Lily Hall!"

"Go ahead, Aunt Lily," said Edward, "stoop over and look aged."

"It isn't as hard as you might think," said Aunt Lily. "Oh, drat it, there's a blot." She sopped up the ink with a corner of the blotter and started adding her column of figures again.

Eleanor looked fondly at Aunt Lily. If you called her a spinster, it didn't seem the right word at all. She was tall and strong and handsome like a Pilgrim woman (or so Eleanor always thought) and she would even have been pretty if her red hair were not pulled back so harshly into a tight bun. Eleanor couldn't remember a time when Aunt Lily had not been the choir-mistress in the big white church around the corner, and when she hadn't taken in piano pupils like washing. Among Eleanor's earliest memories was the familiar sight of Aunt Lily playing the organ in the choir loft of the church, her head pumping vigorously up and down to mark the rhythm for the choir, her hands running nimbly up and down the keyboards, and her feet shifting sideways, heel and toe, to make the deep droning notes of the bass.

Aunt Lily stood up, looking worried, with her

account book in her hand. "Have you seen Uncle Freddy?" she said.

Eleanor knew where Uncle Freddy was, and she decided to include him in her tour. She swept to the parlor arch and pulled back the threadbare curtain. "Behold," she said, "Mr. Frederick Hall! Uncle of our great President! Friend of Emerson! Friend of Thoreau!"

He wasn't really, of course. Emerson and Thoreau had both died long before Uncle Freddy was born. But dear Uncle Freddy was not altogether sound in his mind, and he was confused about this. His heroes and companions were the marble busts of Ralph Waldo Emerson and Henry Thoreau that stood beside the hearth in the parlor. "Waldo" and "Henry" seemed to talk to him, just as he did to them. They had long conversations, and afterwards he would tell everyone what they had said, forgetting that he had read it himself in their books, long ago. He was Aunt Lily's older brother, and he had a kind of absurd dignity that was all his own. His sister and his nephew and his niece were devoted to him.

"Fred, dear," began Aunt Lily.

Uncle Freddy paid no attention. He was banging Thoreau's marble tie. "But Henry, old fellow," he said, "you declare that man is but a grain of sand in the grand broad scheme of Nature? I agree with Waldo that Nature is but the mirror of the soul, a metaphor of the human mind! An allegory! A colossal, thumping gigantic allegory!"

"Fred, dear," said Aunt Lily again.

Uncle Freddy looked around vaguely, his arm around Henry. "What's that?" he said.

Aunt Lily bit her lip. "All right, dear, never mind," she said. She turned and went out again. Eleanor could see that she had gone to Uncle Freddy for help, and then had decided to bear the burden, as always, alone. Eleanor remembered what Miss Prawn had said, "Stark, raving mad, the lot of them! Everybody knows it!" She felt an ache for a minute on behalf of Uncle Freddy, and a strong desire to kick Miss Prawn in the shin. But she shook herself, scowled at Eddy, and went on with her exhibition.

The invisible tourists were very impressed with the statuary in the hall. There was a plaster bust of Louisa May Alcott there, and a hatrack named Mrs. Truth. Both of them, of course, had inspired our great President to higher things. Mrs. Truth was a beautiful life-size bronze lady standing on the newel post at the foot of the stairs. She wasn't a hatrack really, but it was very convenient to throw scarves and umbrella handles over her outflung arm and to hang hats on the book she carried in her hand. And she was inspiring to look at. Her face had classic features and a noble expression. Secretly Eleanor thought she resembled Aunt Lily. Her name came from the word engraved on a sort of bandage across her front. It said "TRUTH." One arm held up a light fixture shaped like a star. The star had a light bulb in it, but there was something the matter with the wiring and it didn't work.

The next wonder to be looked at was the stuffed peacock, Percival, on the landing. He, too, had been a source of deep inspiration to President Edward P. Hall. His feathers were a little ruffled with age, his neck had a dislocated jog in it, and most of his feathery crest was gone, but he clung proudly with his claws to a tall stand and gave the worn stair carpet an air of grandeur.

Then Eleanor walked upstairs and displayed the bedroom that had been occupied by the President as a boy. The President hadn't made his bed. The President's sister scolded the President. "What about the window we were looking for?" said the President, changing the subject. "Where do you suppose it is?"

"It must be in the attic," said Eleanor. She led the way along the balcony and up the attic stairs. At the top of the stairs they came out into the complicated hugeness of the attic, with its octagonal and circular spaces where towers projected on the outside. The floor was cluttered with boxes and trunks. There was a dressmaker's dummy at one side, looking ghostly in a black cloth shroud. Edward and Eleanor made a circuit of the attic, looking for the keyhole window. They couldn't find it.

Downstairs someone began playing the piano noisily. It was Mary Jane Broom, one of Aunt Lily's piano pupils, taking her weekly lesson. Edward closed his eyes and thought. "There were the second-floor windows and the attic windows, but I think this one was all by itself on top. There must be another set of stairs, or a ladder."

But they could find neither ladder nor stairs. Then they examined the ceiling. And in one of the round tower openings the ceiling showed a crack. It was a rectangular crack, and at one end of it there was a little ring. Edward poked at the crack with an old snowshoe. The ceiling jiggled, all along the crack. "Hurray," he said, "it's a trap door!" He ran downstairs for a rope, and came back all the way from the cellar two steps at a time. "Do you want to get on my shoulders," he said, "or shall I get on yours? Look, I'll bend over and you stand on my back."

"What for?" said Eleanor.

"To put the rope through the ring, silly. Come on, get on. Ow, ow! Hurry up!"

"There," said Eleanor, getting down with a final

grinding dig of her heavy shoe in Edward's back. The rope was safely through the ring.

"Don't lose the end," said Edward. "There now, let's pull."

They pulled. The crack wobbled, then slammed shut again. They pulled harder. "Watch out!" said Eleanor, dodging back. The crack had been the outline of a set of ladder-steps, folded up in the ceiling. The ladder came down now slowly and smoothly and dropped its bottom step softly at their feet. It was a stairway where there had been no stairway.

Eleanor looked doubtfully up into the darkness at the top. "It's probably just more old trunks up there," she said.

"Probably," said Edward. He looked up, too.

"You go first," said Eleanor, looking at him.

Edward paused, then put his foot on the bottom step. "All right," he said. He climbed sturdily upward. Eleanor watched his plump short legs go up. Hesitantly she began to follow. He paused when his head went over the edge of the crack, and stopped.

Eleanor stopped, too. "Well?" she said.

"I can't see," said Edward. "There, now I'm getting used to it. There's the window. There's . . ." His voice stopped. He stood stock-still.

"Tell me!" demanded Eleanor.

"Oh—" said Edward. His voice caught.

It wasn't like Edward to be surprised by anything. He was matter-of-fact and took things as they were. Eleanor felt herself breathing hard. She twitched his trouser leg. "What, what?" she said.

Silently Edward moved over and made room for Eleanor to stand beside him. Her tall head rose slowly higher than his into the hidden chamber.

She, too, was blinded at first by the dimness. Then the many colors of the great keyhole window blossomed in the dark and gradually illumined the objects in the room. Were there two windows facing one another? No, one was the reflection of the other in a huge mirror that was sunk into the well of an enormous dresser across the room from the window. There was a table, and what was that on the table? Like a castle? It was a castle, a castle made of blocks. And there were chairs and toys, and a little wagon. And what was that on either side of the window? Eleanor's heart bounded into her throat.

It was two narrow beds, and the covers were turned neatly down.

3

THE LOST CHILDREN

*D*OWNSTAIRS THE DISTANT piano scales stopped suddenly and the front door slammed, faint and far away. Mary Jane's lesson was over. Edward and Eleanor found themselves scurrying helter-skelter down the ladderlike steps and walking with stiff but hurrying legs down the attic stairs and along the corridor, down the big front stairs past Percival, and past the darkened star of Mrs. Truth, to brush through the velvet curtain that hung in the parlor-arch, and confront Aunt Lily. She was arranging her music at the piano. They stood and looked at her with drawn frightened faces.

"When is that child going to pay me?" said Aunt Lily. "So many of them are absent-minded about my fifty cents, do you suppose they embezzle it?" Aunt Lily saw their faces. "Why, what's the matter with you two?"

They told her, then, in a nervous rush of words, about the attic room and the hidden steps and the key-hole window, and the beds. Aunt Lily put her hand up to her forehead and sighed. "So you've found it," she said. "I'd hoped I would never have to tell you."

"But you do," said Eleanor.

Aunt Lily looked at them. She brushed back a stray-ing strand of hair and stuffed it into her bun with a sharp hairpin. "I suppose I do," she said. "Wait here." She got up from the piano stool and went upstairs. Edward and Eleanor sat stiffly on the sofa. Presently she came back, with something in her hand.

It was a photograph album. Aunt Lily sat between them and turned the pages slowly. It was one of those old-fashioned albums with a tooled-leather cover. The pictures were mounted in pretty oval frames, only one to a page. Great-aunts and great-uncles looked out at them, splendid in bustles and bonnets and top hats and frock coats, leaning on carpet-covered tables or stand-ing against painted backgrounds of the eruption of Vesuvius.

"That's Father, isn't it?" said Eleanor, stopping the pages at one place with her finger.

"Yes," said Aunt Lily, "that was Arthur when he was

a student at Harvard College. And here's your sainted mother, just before the accident that cost them both their lives." Aunt Lily sighed again and turned the pages. "Here, this is what I was looking for." She smoothed the pages and opened the book out flat. Eleanor and Edward bent over to see.

On the left-hand page was a photograph of a good-looking boy about Eleanor's age. On the right was a matching photograph of a little girl who looked about as old as Edward. She wore a white frock and black stockings, and with the flood of light hair over her shoulders she looked very much like a pretty picture by Reginald Birch in an old *St. Nicholas* magazine.

"Who are they?" said Eleanor.

"Your Aunt Eleanor and your Uncle Edward," said Aunt Lily.

"But—" said Edward.

"But we never heard of them," said Eleanor.

"There were five of us, you see," said Aunt Lily. "Fred was the oldest. Your father, Arthur, was next. I was next. And Edward and Eleanor were the youngest. We called them Ned and Nora. You children were named for them, of course. I was seventeen when our parents died, and after that I had to take care of Ned and Nora and be housekeeper for all of us. But I didn't mind." Aunt Lily smiled sadly. "They were good, happy children."

"But what happened to them?" said Eleanor.

"They disappeared," said Aunt Lily.

"Disappeared?" said Edward and Eleanor together.

"Yes, one day they just—vanished."

"Is that their beds in the tower room?" said Edward.

"Yes," said Aunt Lily. "They took a fancy to that room and took all their treasures up there. I never gave up hope that they would come back some day, so I kept it ready for them, always."

"Do you still?" said Eleanor in awe.

"Yes," said Aunt Lily.

"But it's been so long," said Edward.

"I don't care," said Aunt Lily. Her voice sounded taut. Eleanor didn't know what to say. She looked at the small faces in the album. They were open friendly faces, with a familiar family look. There was something recognizable in the noses and mouths, something Edward-like in the girl's plump legs and freckled face. . . .

Edward turned the page over. "Look," he said, "who's that?"

Aunt Lily glanced at the picture. Then she did something strange. She turned a deep red and shut the book. Then she shook herself a little and looked at Edward. "Well," she said, "it's part of the story, really." She opened the book again and turned the pages to the picture Edward had found. "This is Prince Krishna, son of the Maharajah of Mandracore."

Edward and Eleanor stared. The photograph was of a tall, slender figure in a plain black suit. He wore a turban on his head. His face was the handsomest Eleanor had ever seen, but it looked at the same time modest and thoughtful. He looked every inch a prince, or a Maharajah, or a king, or anything very great or very noble. His hand was resting on a table, on the open pages of a book.

"That's Emerson's *Essays*," said Aunt Lily. She looked steadily at the picture and began quietly to tell them about Prince Krishna. "He was here, you see, in our house, to study about the Transcendentalists with Fred. Perhaps you children didn't know it, but in those days your Uncle Fred was famous all over the world for his books about Emerson and Thoreau. Even Prince Krishna in India had heard about him, and he came all the way across the world to stay with us, here in Concord, to study them with Fred. He lived with us right here in this very house—" Aunt Lily's voice trailed off.

"What does that word mean, Aunt Lily?" said Eleanor.

"What word?" said Aunt Lily. "Oh, you mean 'Transcendentalist'? Well, it just means people like Emerson and Thoreau, here in New England a hundred years ago. Krishna explained it to me once. I'm not sure I got it straight. I think he said the Transcendentalists believed that men's minds were very wonderful, and that they could know all kinds of important things without being taught about them through their eyes and ears—because they were part of something called an Over-Soul. I think that's what he said."

"Without being taught?" said Eddy. "You mean no school?"

"Well, I don't remember anything like that," said Aunt Lily. "I remember he said that there was real meaning in Nature, and that things like clouds and trees could remind us of these wonderful ideas that we know already. And the Transcendentalists didn't think it was important to get rich. They lived very simply. It was something like that. I may have it all wrong."

Eleanor didn't understand. Eddy did. He decided the Transcendentalists didn't believe in school, and he looked at the busts of Henry and Waldo with new respect.

Aunt Lily was looking again at the picture of Prince Krishna. "I used to cook his meals and dust his room and make his bed," she said. "He was so good! Ned and Nora loved him. And he made up wonderful games for them—treasure hunts with lovely prizes. He was fabulously rich, and the children would find jewels, real rubies and diamonds, tucked in their pockets! But he was like the Transcendentalists—he didn't care about money. He lived in a bare room, and he wouldn't even let me hang curtains in it. And he wore threadbare clothes and sewed on his own bu-buttons!" Aunt Lily broke down, suddenly, and wept.

Eleanor stared. Aunt Lily must have been in love with Prince Krishna! Eleanor couldn't blame her. He was much better-looking than Benjamin Parks. "But what happened to him?" she said.

Aunt Lily recovered herself and straightened up. "He disappeared, too," she said. Her voice sounded flat.

Edward had a brilliant idea. "He kidnapped them! He kidnapped Ned and Nora and took them back to India!"

"No, no," said Aunt Lily. "He didn't disappear until afterwards. They vanished first, and he was just as brokenhearted as the rest of us. The police made a tremendous effort to find them. They searched the town, and they sent detectives all over the country and even all the way to India. But Prince Krishna kept insisting that they were here! Right in this house! He nearly went out of his mind. He ransacked the house, from top to bottom, looking in the most absurd places. He kept saying, 'They MUST be here! They MUST be here!' And then, suddenly, he was gone, too. He never even wrote a letter, not a single line."

A tear fell on the page. Aunt Lily hastily wiped it

away with a fold of her skirt. "And after that your Uncle Freddy was never quite the same."

There was a dried rose pressed between the pages of the album. Aunt Lily picked it up, to catch the scent of an ancient time. "Look, Aunt Lily, who's that?" said Eleanor. On the opposite page, where it had been hidden under the flower, there was a photograph of a young girl, charming and fresh-faced, with a big bow in her long hair, and a shirtwaist and long skirt.

Aunt Lily blew her nose. "Believe it or not," she said a little grimly, "that was me."

"Oh, but she was so pretty!" said Eleanor, gushing over the picture. Then she could have bitten off her tongue. She looked up aghast at Aunt Lily. Aunt Lily said nothing. "Oh, Aunt Lily, not that you're not pretty, too! You're just—just—"

"Old?" suggested Aunt Lily.

"No, of course not," said Eleanor loyally.

"Well," said Aunt Lily, laughing suddenly and getting up. "I'm old enough to hold the whiphand around here. Now you two get busy and do your chores."

Edward stood up slowly. "Where were they when you saw them last—Ned and Nora, I mean?" he said.

"They were in those beds upstairs," said Aunt Lily. "I tucked them in myself, the night before. And in the morning they were gone."

4

THE WRITING ON THE WINDOW

*T*HE SUNSHINE NEXT morning was so bright and honest and normal that Edward and Eleanor felt very brave about going back to the hidden chamber. They climbed up the ladder-steps courageously and poked their red heads over the edge of the trap door.

The little room was altogether different. Sunlight was pouring in through the keyhole window. Instead of being frightening, the furnishings and the small beds looked inviting, friendly, welcoming.

They climbed the rest of the way and stood up in the room. They walked around, they bounced on the beds and examined the toys. Then the keyhole window itself drew them closer. It was very large, filling the space between floor and ceiling. The square bottom section could be raised and lowered like an ordinary sash. It was made of clear glass. The huge round upper part was put together from many pieces of stained glass, colored and mottled in the fashion of a bygone day. In the middle, fitting a little unevenly, there was a great lump of clear glass shaped like a gigantic gem, its rounded surface cut into many facets. It was so thick that it thrust out from the flat plane of the window, projecting into the room a full inch.

"Look at that diamond!" said Edward.

"It's not a diamond, silly," said Eleanor. "It's just glass. A diamond that size would be worth a million dollars, maybe more."

"Well, it looks like a diamond to me," said Edward. Eleanor had to admit that it was a very brilliant piece of glass cutting. Each of its faces seemed to reflect one of the colors of the many-colored window, and to gather them and blend them and pour them back again in one great ray of clear white light.

From that moment on, whenever they referred to it they called it "the diamond." Edward forgot instantly that it was only glass, and Eleanor had to keep reminding herself that she knew, of course, that it was not a diamond. Why, if it were real, they could sell it for at least nine hundred thousand dollars, which would be enough to pay back taxes and paint the house, and Aunt Lily could stop giving piano lessons, and—but, of course, it was only glass.

Edward was fascinated next by the block castle. It was made of old-fashioned "Anchor" blocks. The little cubes and arches and columns and roofing pieces looked just like cut stone and brick and slate, but they were really made in molds from white and red and blue cement. The set of blocks that had been used to build the castle must have been the very biggest and most expensive kind, for the castle was enormous. Its walls and turrets and courtyards and towers covered the surface of the table.

Under the table was a large wooden box. "Look," said Edward, "here's the box the blocks came in." He pulled it out. Inside it there were booklets with pictures that showed how to build old-fashioned railroad stations and lighthouses and "monastery portals" and "belvederes" and "mausoleums." Eddy's fingers itched to tear down the castle and build a lighthouse.

"Oh, see what it says on the cover!" said Eleanor.

She had found the lid of the box. Pasted on it was a small white card, and written on the card in a delicate hand were the words,

For Ned and Nora,
from their devoted
friend—Krishna

"Oh, where are they all?" said Eleanor. Some way, somehow, Ned and Nora must be brought back to this house again, to sleep in their beds and play with their blocks once more—and Prince Krishna must come back to marry Aunt Lily, and to make up games for Ned and Nora again. Then she and Eddy could join in the games, and perhaps they, too, would find diamonds and rubies in their pockets! It was from this room that the lost children had disappeared. The trail must begin here!

Eddy was opening the drawers of the enormous dresser with its tall mirror. Eleanor helped him. They were all empty. Then they looked at the wooden cart resting its shafts in the corner. It was a dogcart, only big enough for dolls. But there were no dolls, unless you counted the armless, legless one in the toybox in the corner. "A basket-case," jeered Edward, when Eleanor picked it up and looked at it.

"Poor thing," said Eleanor, cooing at it.

Next to the doll's box was a bookcase. Leaning against it were two homemade fishing rods. On top of it was a white clay bubble pipe, and next to the bubble pipe was a large seashell. Inside the bookcase there was nothing but books, except for a long narrow box on the bottom shelf.

"What's that?" said Edward. He took it out and looked at it. There were two round holes in the top, and several strings ran across it from end to end. But the strings hung limp. Puzzled, Eddy put it back.

Eleanor was looking at the books. They were the same old familiar "Concord authors"—Thoreau, Emerson, Louisa May Alcott. Eleanor was glad to see Louisa's books there, because they were banished from the library downstairs. Uncle Freddy couldn't stand them. He called Louisa "a sentimental old girl," and he was always threatening to smash her plaster bust. Louisa's poor, chipped, yellowed head was not even allowed in the same room with Henry's and Waldo's but had to stand forlornly in the hall with no one to talk to at all—except a sympathetic Eleanor. Eleanor loved her, and she loved her books, and she was terribly proud of living so near to "Orchard House," where Louisa had lived when she wrote *Little Women*. Nora must have loved her, too!

It was then that Edward discovered something interesting about the window. There were scratches on the clear glass pane. He looked closer. They were words, English words, inscribed on the glass in patterned groups like the verses of a poem. The writing was spidery and fine. He showed it to Eleanor, but she couldn't focus on it with her astigmatic eyes. "You read it," she said.

Edward spelled it out. He had trouble with the first word of the title, which was "Transcendental," but no trouble at all with the second. It was "Treasure"! Laboriously he worked his way through the poem. He was used to reading only print and his own fat round script, and the going was hard. Eleanor mumbled the words after him, and found herself becoming more and more excited. Here is what Edward read—

TRANSCENDENTAL TREASURE

> *This is the keyhole's key*
> *To treasures transcendental:*
> *Objects symbols are*
> *Of abstracts monumental;*
> *The Over-Soul sublime*
> *In everchanging forms*
> *Repeats one truth divine*
> *To man in Nature's terms.*

30

Edward boggled at the strange words. "What is it all about?" he said. But the rest of the verses were easier—

> *The first one is a harp*
> *That plays angelic chords;*
> *Its music sings a tune*
> *Too deep and high for words.*
>
> *The second is a doll-child,*
> *Possessed by one of four,*
> *Fit for any princess*
> *To mother and adore.*
>
> *Living in his Eden,*
> *Playing on his flute,*
> *Henry hoed his beans*
> *And wore an old suit;*
> *Find the third in Walden,*
> *Find it if you will—*
> *Pearls from Coromandel,*
> *Diamonds from Brazil!*
>
> *A mirror shall reflect*
> *What your tomorrows hold.*
> *A treasure it will give*
> *From its infinitude.*

Twinkle, little stars,
Like diamonds in the sky!
You can bring them down,
If you learn how to fly.

The sixth one is a ruby;
Flawless shall it glow,
Love itself the giver
For a bride of snow.

The seventh is a treasure
Rounded by the sea—
Deep and dark it lies;
You can set it free!

A treasure made of ivory,
A palace for the soul.
Melodious marble halls
A treasure map enfold.

The last one is a treasure
Too precious to be bought,
As perfect and as fair as
The crystal sphere of thought.

Eye of bird, eye of fowl,
Hides the treasure chest.
Transcendental jewels . . .

"Which—of—them—is—best?" finished Edward.

He leaned back and rubbed his eyes, while Eleanor said some of the words over to herself: "A doll fit for a princess, pearls, diamonds, rubies, treasure chest, jewels!" She clapped her hands. "Jewels, jewels! It's a treasure hunt for jewels!"

Eddy picked up the lid of the block box and held it up to the window. He was comparing the message written on the card by Prince Krishna with the verses scratched into the glass. "The f's are the same," he said. "See? The bottom loop is backwards. And they both have the same fancy r's. You're right! Prince Krishna must have written the poem, so it's Prince Krishna's treasure hunt!"

Eleanor paced up and down with her hands behind her back, a gesture borrowed from Uncle Freddy. "He made up the treasure hunt for Ned and Nora," she said. "Only instead of hiding candy and toys he hid real treasures—rubies and pearls and diamonds, the way Aunt Lily said! Do you know how rich Maharajahs are? They live in palaces of solid gold!" Eleanor whirled around at Edward and stamped her foot. "Let's find them! If we

33

find just one or two of the treasures, we'll be rich, too!"

Eddy jumped up and down and shouted, "Jewels! Jewels!"

It must have been the vibration of the stamping and jumping that did it. There was a sudden whirring noise, and something flew at Eddy, knocking him perilously near the open trap door. Eleanor shrieked, and saved him from falling through it by grabbing him wildly, dropping on one elbow and scraping off the skin.

In one corner of the room, where it had been thrown into deep shadow, there was something they had not seen before. It was an enormous Jack-in-the-box. It had suddenly burst open and thrown itself at Edward, with a horrid lunging spring. Up and down, now, it recoiled upon itself, lashing violently back and forth, throbbing its great nose upon the floor. At last it stopped, and Edward went over to it cautiously and lifted up its ugly head.

"Oh," said Eleanor, covering her face with her fingers and looking through them, "isn't it horrible!"

The Jack-in-the-box had a terrible face. There was a great hooked nose which almost met an upward hooking chin. The eyes were surrounded with black shadows, and the wide mouth was extended in a frightful grin, with jagged teeth under a black mustache. It leered at them. There still seemed to be a ghost of tense vibrating life in its spring, and it escaped Edward's fingers and flopped forward again at him, hitting him hard. The head was as heavy as lead.

Something about it disturbed Eleanor. She pointed at the cloth wound about the head. "Isn't that a sort of turban?" she said.

"Yes," said Edward, "like the ones they wear in India." He pushed the Jack back upon itself and jammed it into its box and shut the lid. It seemed to want to burst out again, and he had to kneel on the lid, and hold it down with both hands. "Hook it, will you?" said Edward.

Eleanor hooked it, clumsily, and then they climbed slowly down the ladder-steps. She knew, now, why she was so disturbed. There was a funny kind of resemblance between the Jack and the picture of Prince Krishna. Yet the Jack looked all-bad, and Prince Krishna all-good.

All-good? He was, wasn't he?

5

THE SEARCH BEGINS

I T WAS A GLORIOUS MORNING. Eleanor leaned on the kitchen window sill. She saw Mr. LaRue coming along the street, a trash barrel wallowing in front of him. Mr. LaRue was a carpenter and handyman. The cool morning breeze, remarkable for the first day of July, was stirring the stately branches of Concord's lofty elms. Along Walden Street the elms stood like tall vases in which someone had arranged long leafy boughs.

Eleanor felt rhapsodic. "Oh, beautiful elm trees!" she said. "Oh, beautiful, for spacious skies! Oh, beautiful Mr. LaRue! Oh, beautiful whiskers of Mr. LaRue!" The rosy morning light was shining on Mr. LaRue's good-humored old face and lighting up his resplendent handlebar mustache. He walked bowlegged and turned up the path that led to the barn, trundling his empty barrel.

Uncle Freddy was already out. He was supposed to be weeding the vegetable patch, but when he saw Mr. LaRue coming he started to frisk about. Mr. LaRue was used to Uncle Freddy. He stopped politely and lifted his hat. Then he turned his barrel upside down and sat on it. Eleanor ran out-of-doors and leaned her elbows on the silver gazing globe.

"Tell me, Mr. LaRue," said Uncle Freddy, "what is written on the wind?" He cocked his head up and put his hand behind his ear, as though he were listening to the breeze. Mr. LaRue listened, too, then hunched his shoulders. *He* didn't know.

"Henry knows!" said Uncle Freddy. "And so does Waldo!" He jumped up on a tree stump and pointed his finger fiercely at Mr. LaRue. "Oh, mortal!" he said, "thy ears are stones!" Mr. LaRue looked worried and pulled at his big ears. They felt the same as ever, and he looked relieved. But Uncle Freddy still glared at him accusingly.

Oh, (Mr. LaRue) call not Nature dumb!

(recited Uncle Freddy),

These trees and stones are audible to me . . .
. . . The wind,
That rustles down the well-known forest road—

37

It hath a sound more eloquent than speech—

Uncle Freddy jumped suddenly off the stump and made a lunge at the vegetable garden. He pulled lustily at a carrot top, and when it came up too suddenly, he rolled over backwards. Mr. LaRue set him gently back on his feet. Uncle Freddy was waving the muddy carrot in front of his eyes. It was a funny one, with two orange legs, like a man.

"Brother!" cried Uncle Freddy. "Kinsman!" He was talking to the carrot. Eleanor giggled. Then he introduced the carrot to Mr. LaRue, who tipped his hat again and shuffled politely.

"Immense unity," groaned Uncle Freddy. Then he put his arm around Mr. LaRue and dangled the carrot in front of him, discussing it as if he were telling Mr. LaRue about their new mutual friend. "We are all made of one hidden stuff, Mr. LaRue! What is a tree but a rooted man? The elm tree thinks the same as me! So does my friend and brother, here!" Uncle Freddy took a huge muddy bite out of the carrot, then stuck what was left of it in his frayed lapel and smiled triumphantly.

Mr. LaRue picked up his ashcan and rolled it noisily away. He enjoyed listening to Uncle Freddy. It gave him a kind of mysterious good feeling, like church, only out-of-doors, in the sunlight.

Eleanor ran to look for Eddy. Today they were determined to find at least one or two of the hidden jewels, even if it was just one or two pearls or a small ruby. She found him at work in the tower room. He was copying the mystic verses into his notebook, squinting at them and writing carefully, with his tongue between his teeth. He finished, and together they pored over what he had written. Then they spent the rest of the day searching for clues.

First they cudgeled their brains over the "harp that plays angelic chords." Eleanor could see it clearly in her mind. It would be a great gold carved one, with a thousand strings! "They're very valuable, I know that," she said. But they couldn't think where to look. For a while they wandered vaguely around the attic, but there weren't any boxes or trunks there nearly big enough to contain such a gigantic musical instrument. So they gave up on that for the moment and looked farther down the list of treasures.

Eleanor's attention fastened on the doll "fit for a princess." How lovely it would be! Surely it would have golden hair and beautiful silken dresses? Perhaps it would look like a princess itself! She went off on an expedition of her own, groping through Aunt Lily's trunks, making a mess of the linens and winter clothing. But she came away empty-handed, smelling faintly of mothballs.

Edward, too, had been unsuccessful. He had been unable to find the mirror that hid a treasure. Starting with the mirror in the tower room, he had pushed up and down and sideways on moldings in a search for secret hiding places, he had shoved big mirror-topped dressers away from walls to look behind them, and he had stood on his head in front of them to look at himself upside-down. Short of prying the wooden backs off them to see if thousand-dollar bills were hidden under the silvered glass, he didn't know anything else to do.

Some of the verses were so puzzling they didn't know where to begin. How could they learn to fly in order to bring down the diamonds in the sky? The treasure rounded by the sea lay somewhere "deep and dark." Where was that? And who and where was the bride of snow?

Then Eleanor had a bright idea about the last verse. "Eye of bird, eye of fowl, hides the treasure chest—" What about Percival? He was a bird, he was a fowl! She went straight to the peacock on the stair-landing and looked carefully at his eyes. They were small hard black beads. Maybe one was a button, and if you pressed it, the peacock would open his mouth and jewels would pour out. She tried it. Nothing happened.

She tried pressing, twisting and squeezing both eyes at once. Then she got a knitting needle and gouged the eyes out altogether, apologizing under her breath to Percival all the while. They came out easily enough. Underneath each of them was just a hollow socket into which it had fitted—a socket lined with dried glue. Eleanor pushed her finger hard on the insides of the sockets. Nothing happened. Then she tipped Percival over and sat down on the steps with his head in her lap. Carefully and ruthlessly she cut the stitches along the top of his head with her sewing scissors, and pulled his poor moth-eaten skin back. The inside of his head was just a wooden knob covered with cotton padding. Eleanor took the padded knob out, shook it, squeezed it, and then hurriedly stuffed it back in and sewed up Percival's head again, as carefully as she could. Then she glued his eyes back in with paste and stood back to look at him. Was he all right again? There was something a little staring and cross-eyed about him now. "I'm sorry, Percival," mumbled Eleanor, and went off feeling guilty and hoping Aunt Lily wouldn't notice.

Meanwhile Edward had the third treasure all figured out. There must be a chest of jewels, like a pirate chest, at the bottom of Walden Pond! They would have to hire a rowboat and explore the bottom with a huge net or a long hook. He had heard a rumor that the middle of Walden Pond was bottomless. In that case perhaps they could hire a diver. Of course Trebor Nosnibor was the sort of fellow who would go down into the fathomless depths himself! But even Trebor would have to have a diving suit. Perhaps they should find some of the other jewels first and then use the money from them to invest in the boat and the diving gear.

But where were the other jewels? By suppertime Edward and Eleanor were thoroughly discouraged. The game didn't seem so much fun after all. The clues were too hard! Perhaps Ned and Nora had been given a second set of clues to help them. Or perhaps they had just been smarter.

After supper their gloom increased. Aunt Lily had taken on a whole new set of evening piano pupils, and from now on Edward and Eleanor were going to have to wash the supper dishes all by themselves. They were slow about it, the first time. When the last pot was put to soak, Eleanor went to the parlor curtain and peeked through.

Timothy Shaw was taking a lesson. Timothy was a member of Aunt Lily's church choir. He had a very good tenor voice, but he wasn't really interested in playing the piano. He had started taking lessons because he was sweet on Aunt Lily. He was fumbling and bumbling badly. Aunt Lily was severe, Timothy was abject. At last he went home, after lingering for a long time in the doorway and then almost falling down the front steps, saying good-bye. Aunt Lily came into the kitchen and leaned wearily against the sink. "Oh, dear," she said.

Terrible words rose up from the cellar. Eddy was down there, having a last look around for clues. Aunt Lily called down the stairs, "What did you say?"

Eddy answered in an angry roar, "I said a swear!"

"That's what I thought," said Aunt Lily. "Whatever is the matter?"

"I dropped the toolbox on my toe!" bellowed Edward.

Aunt Lily dealt with the wounded toe. Eddy was sore, Eleanor was glum. Aunt Lily was pale and tired.

"I don't suppose," said Eleanor suddenly, "you'd let us sleep in the tower room?"

Aunt Lily put her hand to her head and tried to think about it. Why not, after all? The thing that had happened there was very long ago. "Well, go ahead," she said.

Delighted, Edward and Eleanor decided to go to bed right away. They put on their night clothes hurriedly, and climbed the attic stairs and the ladder-steps. They jumped into the small beds. Excitedly they leaned on their elbows and looked out of the window. It was thrilling to be up so high, in their own secret place! The street lights far below shone around the edges of the huge leafy elm trees. The breeze that had freshened the morning was still playing with their smaller branches, lifting them gently and letting them go again.

Away across the Mill Brook there were window lights. "You can see Emerson's house from here," said Edward.

"His ghost is walking!" said Eleanor.

"It's just the caretaker," said Edward.

Eleanor, drifting off to sleep, found herself thinking of something Uncle Freddy had said, when he was talking to Mr. LaRue—"The elm tree thinks the same as me." What did it mean? She had a funny picture of old Ralph Waldo Emerson standing in his front yard talking on a crank-up telephone that was attached to the trunk of an elm, and the elm tree talking back to him, and nodding its head and agreeing.

And into the room the diamond shed its own faceted light, gathered from the street lights, and the starlight, and the windows of Emerson's old house. Softly the light shone over the two children's beds, and over the possessions of Ned and Nora, and over the slumbering faces of Eleanor and Edward.

6

THE ANGELIC HARP

THEY STOOD AT THE bottom of an elm tree. It was perfectly enormous. It was easy to see why it looked so big. They were very small. It was delightful to be small! "Come on," said Edward, "let's climb."

Ned and Nora were looking for the treasure, too. They were already high up in the branches, far overhead. Eleanor and Edward could hear them laughing and calling to one another. Edward put his foot on a knotted root, sought for handholds in the ridged bark, and started to climb. Eleanor followed him close behind.

The going was easy. The trunk of the tree was knobbed and channeled in grooves, and there were networks of ribs between the grooves. They climbed lightly and quickly, and before long they were high above the ground.

The voices of Ned and Nora beckoned them on, and now and then, through hollow openings between branches, they caught glimpses of a red head, or a scrap of white dress, or a dangling leg. Up and up they climbed, tirelessly. At last they found themselves at a place where the huge trunk separated, and a tremendous limb split off, like a thumb projecting from a hand. They rested in the hollow for a while, and then climbed on. The main stem rose higher and then split into long fingering branches. Which way had the lost children gone? Their voices seemed to come from different places, now on this side, now on that.

Eleanor didn't care very much whether they found them or not, she was enjoying the climbing itself so much. It was as easy as going upstairs. The shaggy bark offered steps and leaning-places and outthrust chairs to sit on. She planned to climb to the topmost branch and blow around with the wind. Then, swaying back and forth, she would just let go and fly away! Just fly away, and soar and float all the way down to the ground!

They were resting again. What was Eddy saying? He was turning his head from side to side. "Listen," he said, "what's that noise?"

"What noise?" said Eleanor. She listened. Ned's and Nora's voices seemed to have stopped. Eddy lay down full-length on the branch and put his ear to the bark. "It's inside," he said. Eleanor lay down, too, and listened.

"So it is," she said. There was a sound inside the tree. There was a murmur, rising and falling, like voices talking in another room, and a sense of something flowing, moving, racing. "What are they saying?" said Eleanor. She thought that if she could just get her ear a little closer she would be able to make out the words.

Eddy sat up and poked his finger at the bark. If only he had a jackknife, he could carve out a hole in the branch and put his ear to that. Surely then he would be able to hear! He knew just the kind of jackknife he wanted. It should have a lot of different blades for doing different kinds of things. Trebor Nosnibor would have a knife like that hanging on his belt, ready for anything, any time, anywhere.

They climbed on again. The overarching crown of the tree was directly above them. The branch they were climbing had tapered down until it was so narrow Edward and Eleanor could wrap their arms and legs around it. The top of the elm tree was like a world in itself, and each of its main branches was like a minor continent supporting a vast population of leaves. The leaves themselves had voices, soft ones. They brushed and stroked against one another, and nodded and bowed and rippled and rustled, their interleaving gently stirred by the breeze. It sounded like whispered conversation. Eleanor and Edward listened, but again the murmuring was too muffled to be heard as words and speech.

"Perhaps," thought Eddy, "it's Backwards English!" He strained all his attention at turning the soft leafy phrases around. But it didn't work. The tree spoke another language entirely.

Then they heard another sound. It was coming from below them, and they leaned sideways to find its source. There it was, hanging on a lower branch, a long narrow box with two holes in the front. It was strung up and down with strings, and across the strings the wind was blowing, making a wonderful strumming noise. They had found the treasure! It was the harp, the harp in the poem, and the music that it made was like a translation of the voices of the tree into some simple and wordless language of the mind. They understood, then, what the tree was saying, and for a while they sat quietly, just listening to it. But then, without warning, the wind changed.

The wind-harp tossed back and forth, and gave out a strident, shrill sound as gusts blew across its strings. The branch upon which Edward and Eleanor were leaning rocked sickeningly. Edward was flung backwards and lost hold with his hands, but his knees were locked and he hung on. The gusts came again, and then again, more and more violently.

"It's only a dream," thought Eleanor desperately, as the branch lashed up and down. She was one of those unlucky ones who become seasick very easily, and the sensations of wild rising and bottomless dropping were very unpleasant. Could she hang on? She knew, somehow, that she would not "fly away and soar," if she let go—she would drop like a stone. Foolish dream! Silly nightmare! Why didn't she hurry and wake up? The long boughs of the elm tree were creaking and groaning and grinding dangerously against one another. Eleanor despaired. And all at once the wind won.

She was knocked off by the downlashing of an upper branch, and found herself catching at air and dropping with frightening speed. Downward she fell, snatching at leaves. They tore away, but each handful checked her speed a little, and then she caught one that tore apart only slowly, so that she was able to dangle from it long enough to look frantically around. Then with a great twist and wrench of her body she sent herself falling in a different direction. Had she judged correctly? With a scraping, thrashing plunge she fell against the wind-harp, and grasped its strings. Secure at last, she hung on, then climbed and squeezed around them, and wormed her way inside one of the round holes. She was bruised pretty well everywhere, and bleeding from a long scratch on her leg. Nothing serious. She stood up in the bottom of the wind-harp and stuck her head out of the hole.

Eddy was coming. The wind had died down again, and he was groping his way along the branches that led to her perch. At last he slipped in beside her. She showed him her scratch. Then she woke up. The dream was over.

Eleanor sat bolt upright. It was morning. She must tell Eddy about her dream!

But Eddy was already up. He was padding across the floor in pajamas that were too big for him.

"Oh, Eddy," said Eleanor, "I had the funniest dream! Wait till you hear—" She stretched her arms over her head and yawned. Oh, oh, why did she hurt so much? What had she done yesterday that had left her so black and blue?

Eddy was jumping up and down. "Hurray!" he said. "I found it! I found the harp! Look, it's right here, the first treasure!" He was holding in his hands the long box that had lain on the shelf of the bookcase. Sure enough, there were the two holes and the set of strings. It was just the same. "It was in the tree—" said Eddy.

"And the wind blew," said Eleanor, hopping out of bed. "And I fell off—" The pain from her bruises and the meaning of what Edward was saying struck her at the same time. "Oh, oh, no," she said, bending over, "oh, Eddy, that was my dream! You can't get into my dream!"

Edward was staring at her, his round face blank. "There was a big elm tree," he said slowly.

"Yes," said Eleanor, "and you and I were climbing it, looking for the treasure, and Ned and Nora were in the tree—"

Edward nodded solemnly, and Eleanor looked at him and started to laugh. His red hair was so tousled it was standing up straight, and his rumpled pajama-legs trailed behind him on the floor. It was ridiculous. It just couldn't be possible. Eleanor sat on her bed and rolled from side to side, laughing. That hurt so much that she stopped and sat up. But if it was just a dream, why was she so black and blue? Then Eleanor lifted the hem of her nightgown and looked at her bare calf.

There was a vicious red scratch running from her ankle to her knee. . . .

7

THE BLOOD OATH

*I*T WAS SUNDAY MORNING. Aunt Lily was in church playing the organ and conducting her choir. Uncle Freddy had gone with her to listen to Mr. Patterson's sermon. (He had promised Aunt Lily faithfully that he would not bob up in the middle to lecture the congregation about Waldo and Henry, because that was very hard on poor Mr. Patterson.)

Edward and Eleanor brought the wind-harp downstairs to the kitchen. Aunt Lily had left breakfast ready. They sat soberly and ate it and puzzled their heads over the meaning of the dream.

"It was real," said Edward.

"No," said Eleanor, "I think it was a dream all right.

But what happens to you in a dream like that happens to you for good, it lasts forever."

"Then that explains what happened to Ned and Nora, and maybe to Prince Krishna, too," said Edward. "They were caught in a dream! Ned and Nora were in our dream, weren't they?"

Eleanor pondered. "I think we were having the same dream last night that Ned and Nora had a long time ago. You see, the dream was a clue to the first of Prince Krishna's treasures—the harp. The dream led us to it, and we found it."

"But Ned and Nora found it, first."

"It must have been hanging in the tree, when they found it. They woke up and went outdoors and climbed the tree and brought it down." Eleanor wrinkled her brow. "Do you suppose the wind blew hard on them, too?" She thought about it. "Well, anyway, we know they woke up, all right, and found the harp. Whatever it was that finally happened to them, it must have happened during another dream, while they were looking for another treasure. Oh, Eddy, maybe we *can* find them! Or at least find out what happened to them!"

"But why," said Edward, "why, if the dream is part of the treasure hunt, would anything *bad* happen in it? If Prince Krishna made the dream happen, and if what happens to you in the dream *really* happens to you, I mean—" Edward was tangled up in his sentence, and he stopped to worry it out.

"Oh," said Eleanor, "I see what you mean." She put her glasses on. Seeing the world sharply always made her brain work better. "You mean, if Prince Krishna had really been a friend of theirs he wouldn't have let a dangerous wind come up in the dream? Maybe it didn't, in *their* dream." Then she had an unhappy thought, and was silent. Or maybe Prince Krishna had been a bad man, and in that case Aunt Lily had been well rid of him!

Aunt Lily breezed in just then, making Eleanor blush for her thoughts. She was singing heartily the words of the final hymn of the morning service, "Oh, for a Faith That Will Not Shrink, Though Pressed by Many a Foe!" Aunt Lily bustled around the kitchen in her rusty black choir robe, heating up a pot of coffee. "I'm always tempted," she said, laughing, "to sing the word 'shirt' instead of 'faith,' it fits in there so well."

Eleanor and Edward relieved their anxiety by joining loudly in this version of the hymn, which Aunt Lily named "The Laundress's Prayer." Then Aunt Lily noticed the wind-harp on the table, and she stopped short. Carefully she set her coffee cup down beside it and strummed her fingers over the strings. Then she sat down and told them about it, haltingly. He had made it. Prince Krishna. For the children. He had hung it in the front yard, in the

54

big elm, for the wind to blow through. Ned and Nora had brought it down to play with. After they were gone, she had put it upstairs with their other treasures.

"Treasures?" said Eleanor and Edward together.

"Well, you know," said Aunt Lily, "their toys and books and things. Oh," she said, "you mean the jewels they found in their pockets? We never could find a sign of them, afterwards. Goodness knows, we could have used a few of them!"

Uncle Freddy came in from church. He was over-joyed to see the wind-harp. "Waldo has one!" he said. "He keeps it in his study window, and the wind blows through it and tells him the secrets of the universe!" The backwash of Uncle Freddy's memory tossed up a verse about Waldo's harp—

> . . . *my minstrel knows and tells*
> *The counsel of the gods,*
> *Knows of Holy Book the spells,*
> *Knows the law of Night and Day,*
> *And the heart of girl and boy,*
> *The tragic and the gay . . .*

Uncle Freddy laid the harp tenderly on the window sill. There was just enough movement of air to bring from the strings a very faint sound, out of key and almost inaudible.

"It needs to be tuned, of course," said Aunt Lily. But to Eleanor and Edward the sound brought back echoes of the tune "too deep and high for words," that they had heard from the harp in their dream. "Come on, Eddy," said Eleanor, getting up suddenly.

She ran into the parlor and picked up the photograph album from the table. Together they looked at the picture of Prince Krishna again. Eleanor studied it closely. Could he have been the worker of evil spells? No, no, it was impossible. Eleanor refused to believe it. Not with that high-browed face and gentle look! She stared again at the picture of Aunt Lily, with her trusting face and the big bow in her hair. Eddy turned the page back to the pictures of Ned and Nora, and together they looked once more at the old brown photographs of the lost children.

Eleanor frowned sternly. "Oh, for a faith that will not shrink, though pressed by many a foe!" She turned her frown on Edward. "Mine won't shrink, no matter how many foes press me!"

"Mine either!" said Edward. "We'll go right on until we find them!"

They signed an oath in blood. "Ouch!" cried Eleanor, when Eddy jabbed her finger with a hatpin. "You didn't have to stick it in so hard. Look at it bleed!"

Edward grinned. "Doolb, doolb," he said, smacking

his lips. "If I had a jackknife with a really sharp blade, you'd never even feel it."

"Thank goodness you don't," said Eleanor crossly, "you'd probably slice my finger right off!" She flapped her wounded hand up and down.

The oath went like this—

We, the undersigned, swear with our blood to discover the whereabouts of Ned and Nora Hall and their friend, Prince Krishna, or die in the attempt. Signed in our heart's blood:

ELEANOR HALL
EDWARD HALL

Eleanor looked at the oath doubtfully. "Do you think we should leave that in about dying in the attempt?" she said.

"Sure," said Edward carelessly, "why not?"

8

MISS PRAWN BARGES IN

UT EDWARD AND ELEANOR had no more dreams
for a while. And when they did, the dream was a
pretty, harmless one. Afterwards, Eleanor
decided it must have been invented just for Nora. It
began with the wedding Eleanor was arranging.

She was marrying Louisa May Alcott's bust to Henry
Thoreau's. It had struck her one day that Louisa had been
a spinster in real life, and Henry a bachelor. And wasn't
there something soft and pleading in Louisa's plaster
eyes? Wasn't there something manly and highly attrac-
tive, too, in Henry's marble good looks? Eleanor decided
that they had been deeply in love for the better part of a
century and ought to be married without further delay.

Waldo would marry them, of course. He had been a clergyman once, so that worked out just right. But first Eleanor chaperoned their wooing. She wrote pining love letters for each of them and delivered them back and forth, from parlor to front hall, reading them aloud softly to the recipients like a dutiful duenna. Uncle Freddy wouldn't approve, of course, so Eleanor conducted the romance when he wasn't there.

When Henry's avowals of undying love had won a bashful acceptance from Louisa, Eleanor prepared for the ceremony. She gathered some wild flowers and put them in a glass on the parlor table. She lighted candles. She tipped Louisa May dangerously over to roll on the edge of her columnar base into the parlor, and stand beside Henry. It was too bad that Louisa's bust was larger than life-size—it towered several inches over Henry's. He looked dignified but somewhat overpowered beside her. Eleanor found an old piece of net and draped it tenderly over Louisa's large bun. It covered the chipped place on the top of her head, but not the one on her nose. Better bring it forward, just far enough to hide the chip. Now, did a few daisies arranged on top of the veil help, or did they look too fussy? They were *lovely*, Eleanor decided, standing back and clasping her hands. Louisa looked almost pretty!

Next to roll Waldo into position. There was a terrible

moment when she discovered almost too late that he was not fastened to his base, and he almost teetered off it. After a wild series of wobbles and counter-wobbles, he jiggled serenely back into position, smiling all the while his saintly smile. Eleanor bumped him across the floor carefully, until he faced the tender couple.

"Tum *tum* ta *tum*," sang Eleanor. She played a few chords on the piano. Then she got up and talked in a deep, rich voice for Waldo—"We are gathered here today to join in the bonds of holy matrimony this man and this woman. Do you, Louisa, solemnly swear to love, honor, and obey your husband, till death do you part?"

"I do," said Louisa shyly.

"Do you, Henry," said Waldo, "promise to love, honor, and cherish this woman till death do you part?"

Henry was about to answer, when Uncle Freddy suddenly parted the curtains and burst in. His eyes goggled at the sentimental scene.

"I forbid it! I forbid this union!" he cried. "My poor Henry! They would never get along!" He snatched off Louisa's veil. Then he picked her up and carried her bodily back out into the hall, staggering under her weight. He set her down with a bang that jarred more chips off her nose. Then he glared at Eleanor and marched off in wrath.

Eleanor burst into tears. She put her arms around Louisa to console her. "Never you mind," wept Eleanor, "don't you cry. There are other fish in the sea besides that old Henry! Just because he lived in a house in the woods by Walden Pond and wrote a book about it, Uncle Freddy thinks he's wonderful!" Eleanor stroked Louisa's chipped nose. "Why, I'll bet you wrote twice as many books as he did, and I'll bet about a million people read your books every day! I'll bet a million girls my age are reading *Little Women* right now, somewhere in the world!"

Eleanor felt soothed. That was fame! That was glory! Just to prove her loyalty to Louisa, she went upstairs to the tower room and found Nora's copy of *Little Women* and came back downstairs with it. She sat down on the floor in front of Louisa May Alcott's plaster bust. Ostentatiously she opened the book and started to read.

She had read only five sentences, when she looked up at Louisa, her mind alive with an idea. This was the fifth sentence: "The four young faces on which the firelight shone brightened at the cheerful words. . . ."

"Four young faces!" Eleanor said over to herself the mystic verse from the window: "'The second is a doll-child, Possessed by one of four, Fit for any princess to mother and adore. . . .'"

Could it be that in Orchard House there was a beautiful doll that had belonged to one of the four Alcott girls? Eleanor slammed the book shut. She was sure of it. *Little Women* was the story of Meg, Jo, Beth, and Amy March, but Eleanor knew that much of the story had been taken from the real life of Louisa May Alcott, who had done part of her growing up in Concord, just over yonder on Lexington Road! The doll must have been hers! It might still be there, preserved forever for the eyes of visiting tourists. But it was the treasure! Nora's treasure! Eleanor's treasure! How could she get it back?

To get into Orchard House she would have to have money. It was a museum now, with a lady guide to show people around. Eleanor told Edward about her plan. He didn't think much of it, but he was the one with the money. It sat on his dresser—seven nickels, thirteen pennies and two dimes, all arranged in a geometrical pattern with sixteen bottle caps, five sugar lumps and twenty-four matchboxes. "I'll have to rearrange everything," said Edward wearily. But he gave in, put the money in his pocket, and went along.

At the door they were met by the guide. They paid their money and joined a group of tourists in Mr. Alcott's library. The others were mostly elderly ladies. They oohed and aahed over everything. The lady guide explained that Mr. Alcott was a close friend of Mr. Emerson's. She pointed out the books and the pictures and the inspiring motto over the fireplace, "The hills are reared, the seas are scooped in vain, if learning's altar vanish from the plain."

Edward began backing up. Ever so casually he backed his way right out of the room. Eleanor backed out, too. Had anyone seen them go? No one seemed to have missed them. Swiftly they looked around the second room. It was full of glass cases—paintings by Louisa's artistic younger sister, who was Amy in *Little Women*, a plaster cast of her foot, a fan—but no doll.

"Come on," said Edward. They wandered freely over the small house, examining the kitchen, the dining room, the parlor. Then they cautiously climbed the stairs and looked around on the second floor.

The party of tourists came upstairs, too, before long. Edward and Eleanor dodged ahead of them, moving swiftly and quietly from room to room. They examined Louisa's room, her sister May's room, Mother Alcott's room. No dolls were to be found. The official party had made its way downstairs again and out the front door, when Eleanor and Edward discovered a little room at the very back of the house that was fitted up for children. There were pieces of small-size furniture in it, and a little iron bedstead and some toys and games.

"There must be a doll here!" said Eleanor. They forgot caution and handled everything. Eleanor lifted the little desk-top and looked inside. Edward began to grope under the mattress of the bed. Then Eleanor found a narrow space filled with old round-topped trunks. She was on her hands and knees unstrapping one of them when she heard a terrible sound. Another party of tourists was approaching. Where had they come from? There hadn't been time for a new party to "do" the downstairs. But here they were! Eleanor froze with her guilty hand inside the trunk.

It was Miss Prawn! She had just walked right in with her own group of ladies! She sailed right past Eleanor and stood in the middle of the room giving a lecture. Eleanor peeked at the large backs of the ladies. One of them was especially stout (she was Miss Prawn's second cousin). Miss Prawn was talking in a sugary voice.

"Oh, my friends," she said, "how reverently do we cherish the memory of our sweet Louisa May, who spent the happiest moments of her dear childhood in our own beloved Concord! She was such a lovely child, so sweet and refined and genteel! What a lesson it is to see the results of a ladylike childhood, the fruit of an educated home! Especially today! Why, I know of two children, almost within the sound of my voice, so wild and ill-mannered you wouldn't believe it!"

Eleanor stayed frozen. Perhaps if she didn't move so much as a hair they might go away without seeing her.

But where was Edward? There was no place for him to hide—no closet, no door—and the little room was a dead-end. Could he have climbed out the window?

Suddenly there was a scream. Then scream after scream! Miss Prawn had sat down on Eddy! He had been lying stiff and flat and still in the bed, with the covers pulled up over his head. He reared up now, and roared, "KCITSMOORB!"

Eleanor decided, with a kind of Doomsday joy, that they might as well be killed for a sheep as for a lamb. She jumped out from behind the trunk. Miss Prawn caught sight of her at once, and her screams went up an octave. Miss Prawn's second cousin was yanking Edward out of bed and shaking him. She gave him a dreadful slap across the face. Eleanor jumped at her and sank her teeth into her arm. Then there was a free-for-all, with Miss Prawn standing in the middle howling, and six large ladies doing battle with two small children. The ladies had weapons in the shape of umbrellas and heavy pocketbooks. The ladies won.

If there was treasure hidden in Orchard House, Eleanor knew now that they would never find it. They were marched angrily home by Miss Prawn's second cousin (Miss Prawn was still having hysterics and couldn't do it herself), the doorbell of the Halls' house was pushed imperiously, and Aunt Lily was given a tongue-lashing. Miss Prawn's second cousin used phrases like "criminal assault" and "parental neglect" and "disgraceful living conditions."

Aunt Lily said she was sorry, and she looked so sad that Eleanor and Edward both felt heartily ashamed at having caused her trouble. As if she didn't have enough of it already!

When Miss Prawn's angry relative had gone, Aunt Lily didn't say anything. She just gave them supper and got ready to leave the house. She was going out in her old car to another town, where she had taken on still more new pupils. She was wearing herself out with teaching, trying to pay the back taxes! She came in to say good-bye while Eleanor was tidying up. She looked a little forlorn, as she buttoned the front of her old black coat. For the first time Eleanor wondered if perhaps Aunt Lily did look a little old. Her nose was red, and so were her eyes, and her hair was pulled back plainly, painfully tight.

"Perhaps I am neglecting you, the way that woman said," said Aunt Lily. She dabbed at her eyes and went out. Eleanor and Edward watched her back her car out of the barn and progress in a stately fashion down the street, her spine straight and her head high. Eleanor suddenly saw her as a mythical heroine, as glorious in her ancient automobile on the way to Acton to give a piano lesson as some Greek goddess with a flowing white gown, riding in a chariot in a picture.

"You're not neglecting us!" said Eleanor to herself, tugging angrily at the dishtowel, "we're neglecting you!"

They *must* find some of the treasure, and soon! Not just for Ned and Nora, but to help Aunt Lily, *now*.

9

THE DOLL-CHILD

ELEANOR WAS LYING ON a huge bed, staring up at the top of a tall door. She knew without thinking about it that she was a doll. She felt strangely stiff in some places and strangely limp in others. Her head and neck had a porcelain solidity, and so did her arms and legs. The rest of her felt like—what? Cotton? No, sawdust! Sawdust solidly packed in cloth. Her dress felt long and old-fashioned, and what was that odd sensation around her porcelain calves? Ruffles? Thinking soberly about it, Eleanor decided that she must be wearing pantalettes. There was a great lumpy button on the back of her dress.

Was she herself the treasure, the doll fit for a princess?

The good thing about these dreams was that there were some things you *knew*. And Eleanor knew that she was not the treasure. Then where was it? Something was lying near her. Was it another doll? Eleanor strained to analyze it out of the corner of her painted eyes.

It was not a doll, but a small fat wooden pony on wheels. One of its wheels was broken and its mane and tail were gone.

"Hello?" said the pony. "Is anyone there?"

It was Edward. "Eddy!" said Eleanor.

"Oh, Eleanor! Is that you?" said the pony. He whinnied. "What a funny-looking doll you are!"

Eleanor was offended. "You're not much to look at yourself," she shot back. "What happened to your tail?"

"I think somebody pulled it right out," said Edward.

Just then the door at which Eleanor was looking so fixedly opened. A large human shape came in and stood over her. Eleanor found herself looking straight up at two eyes. They were part of a pale girlish face.

The face spoke. "Seraphina, dear," it said. Then its huge hand reached out, enveloped Eleanor, and picked her up. Eleanor was frightened, but the hand was careful, and closed high around her waist. The face came close, then rapidly grew smaller, as its owner held her hand out at arm's length to look critically at the doll that was Eleanor-Seraphina.

"You are sadly in need, Seraphina dear, of a little refreshment. Never have I seen you look so pale." A finger came thrusting out of the distance and filled Eleanor's view. It was feeling her forehead. There was a shocked clucking sound from the enormous little girl.

"But you have a fever!" said the little girl. "How long have you been lying here, wasting away with illness, and your wretched mother away from home? Poor, poor child!" Tenderly the huge hands cradled Eleanor.

"Now Guinevere and Elfrida, you must sleep in my bed, and let poor Seraphina have yours," said the girl, stooping down to a wooden box on the floor. With one hand she nestled Eleanor-Seraphina, and with the other she gently removed two doll-invalids from a folded piece of toweling and laid them on the high bed. Eleanor-Seraphina struggled to get a glimpse of Guinevere and Elfrida, but failed. Was one of them the treasure? She herself was being placed delicately in the box, and covered with a clean handkerchief and a scrap of flannel.

"Now, Galahad," said the big little girl, "you must be the doctor." Edward was grasped around the middle and lifted down to the floor, to stand with his wooden nose leaning against the box.

Seen from the floor, the little girl was even more overwhelming. She made the floor tremble, moving about to find medicines for her "sick child." She brought back a scrap of wet cloth to cool Eleanor's china head, and then supported her so that she could click her painted mouth against the edge of a small cup of invisible tonic-tea.

"I know it tastes nasty," said the girl, "but be brave, Seraphina dear."

"Beth! Beth!" There was a thundering noise on the other side of the door, and three more giant girls burst in. Two of them were even more colossal in size than the first. Eleanor's sawdust trembled with fear. Surely she would be stepped on, or crushed!

But it was soon apparent that only one of the giants was to be feared. The first one, Beth, had been all gentleness. The oldest one, Anna, seemed almost grown-up and moved with ladylike dignity. The smallest, May, was cunning and graceful, and flounced her skirts prettily into a chair. But the fourth!

Her name was Louisa. She was very tall. She had brought her hoop, and now she sent it careering and wallowing around the narrow room. It careened against the bed and subsided against the floor with a window-rattling din.

"Loui-SA!" said Anna, the oldest giant girl.

"Oh, Beth," said Louisa, "I've got it perfect! Starting right here at Hillside, I rolled my hoop all the way past

Mr. Emerson's, right down Main Street past the Milldam stores and back again, and all the way down North Road—guess how far?"

"Where, Louisa?" said May, the smallest giant girl. "Not as far as Mr. Proctor's house?"

"Guess again!" said Louisa. She picked up the wooden pony that was Edward and sent him scooting across the floor. His wheels skidded and the broken one threw him off balance. He went banging noisily to a stop on his side. Eleanor couldn't see, but she could hear, and her sawdust insides winced.

"Not as far as the North Bridge!" said Beth.

Louisa was triumphant. "To the North Bridge and across it and right around the bumpy battleground and all the way home again! Without even a wobble!"

Suddenly Louisa scooped her big brown hand into Eleanor's bed and dragged her forth. "Oh, Beth," she said, holding Eleanor-Seraphina high up over her head, "who's sick now?"

Beth jumped up and reached for her sick child. "Oh, please, please, Louisa! That's Seraphina, my best, best doll! Oh, please, don't hurt her!"

"Louisa, do be careful," said Anna.

"Funny old Beth," said Louisa, in a softer voice, "here's your dolly." She tossed Eleanor-Seraphina onto the bed, where she landed with a thump. "And you might as well have this one, too. I've got a new patient for your hospital." Louisa hitched up her pinafore, pulled something out of the pocket of her dress, and began tossing it up in the air and catching it again.

The something was a shapeless rag. Little May jumped out of her chair. "It's not Joanna?" she said.

"What if it is?" said Louisa. "She's had a pretty gay life." She sent Joanna sailing higher and higher, until her poor knobby head thumped against the ceiling.

"Look at her!" said May.

"Oh, Louisa, you terrible girl!" said Anna, laughing. "No wonder Father says you're possessed!" She went out of the room and shut the door, and Louisa laughed, too, and threw the wretched patient on the bed.

Body and head were all there was left of Joanna. Her arms and legs were gone, and her head was bald. Her poor face was so dirty that the features were almost obscured. Beth clucked and cooed over it. She found a cap and tied it over the baldness. Then she wrapped the body in a small blanket and rocked it in her arms.

Louisa pulled a book out of her big pinafore pocket and fell back on the bed. She tugged an apple out of another pocket, and then, for the first time, she stopped creating a commotion. She opened the book, took a big bite out of the apple, and was soon dead to the world. She had flopped right on top of Eleanor-Seraphina, who found herself crushed, smothered, and blinded. May came to Eleanor's rescue. She tugged on her slender china feet and set her up elegantly in the rocking chair, with her hands crossed in her lap.

All at once May's hands stopped arranging the folds of Eleanor's dress, Beth stopped rocking her new invalid, and Louisa sat up on the bed, her apple halfway to her lips. There was a new step on the stair. Eleanor forced all her attention to the corners of her painted eyes, to see who the newcomer might be.

The door opened, and a man came in. He had long light hair and a mild face. "Come, my pure souls," he said, "still at your innocent recreations? The time has come for studies. We must keep to the order of our duties." He stroked Beth's hair. "Prompt, cheerful, unquestioning obedience," he said, with a smile. He patted May's cheek. "Vigilance, punctuality, persever- ance!"

Louisa jumped off the bed with a sigh, and slammed her book shut. The man looked at her sadly, and said softly, "Government of temper, hands, and tongue!" Louisa, subdued, started for the door, but she tripped over the pony that was Edward, and fell down with her whole gangly length on the floor. When she got up there were tears in her eyes. Her father shook his head sor- rowfully. "Gentle manners, my poor Louisa," he said,

"gentle manners, motions, and words!" Then he gathered the three girls before him, followed them out, and
shut the door. The room was empty.

Empty, that is, except for a plain-looking doll with a
china head in the rocking chair by the window, and a
battered wooden pony on the floor. Eleanor-Seraphina
had nothing left to stare at but the opposite wall, and
now that slowly began to fade. Her short life as a doll
was over, and slowly, regretfully, Eleanor woke up to a
new morning in her own bed in the tower room, a full-
sized flesh-and-blood girl again.

She climbed out of bed at once, to find her treasure.
It was in the box in the corner—the armless, legless
doll. Eleanor picked it up tenderly and took it back to
bed with her. She laid its head on the pillow beside her
own and looked at it reverently.

It was Louisa's doll! And the four girls in the dream
were Louisa May Alcott herself and her three sisters,
who were Jo, Meg, Beth, and Amy in *Little Women*. And
poor ragged Joanna was in the book, too! Eleanor
reached for the book, which was beside her bed, found
the place, and read it aloud to Edward, who was yawning
and stretching and rubbing his eyes, only half waked up.

One forlorn fragment of *dollanity* had belonged to
Jo; and, having led a tempestuous life, was left a

75

wreck in the ragbag, from which dreary poorhouse it was rescued by Beth, and taken to her refuge. Having no top to its head, she tied on a neat little cap, and, as both arms and legs were gone, she hid these deficiencies by folding it in a blanket, and devoting her best bed to this chronic invalid. If anyone had known the care lavished on that dolly, I think it would have touched their hearts, even while they laughed.

So that part of *Little Women* had been real! Beth was the one who had died in the book. And that was true, too—the real Beth had died young. She had been the gentle one, and she had really and truly adopted Louisa's old doll! Jo's doll, Beth's doll! Someone in the Alcott family must have given it to some little girl in the Hall family, long ago. And perhaps Aunt Lily had shown it to Prince Krishna. And he had made a treasure of it, for Nora.

Eleanor touched the dirty cheek in awe. No gilded, fluffy-headed doll in the world could compare in preciousness with this "forlorn fragment" of Jo's and Beth's. "Fit for any princess to mother and adore." It was a treasure indeed!

10

DISASTER AT WALDEN

INDING THE DOLL from *Little Women* was a triumph, but it had brought them no closer to Ned and Nora, and the doll Joanna wasn't the kind of treasure that would help Aunt Lily. Eleanor and Edward studied the verses in Edward's notebook again.

"What we want to find is one of the jewels," said Eleanor, "like this ruby here."

"If we could only figure out this verse, we'd have both diamonds *and* pearls," said Edward. He read it aloud—

> *Living in his Eden,*
> *Playing on his flute,*

Henry hoed his beans
And wore an old suit;
Find the third in Walden,
Find it if you will!
Pearls from Coromandel,
Diamonds from Brazil!

"Do you suppose," said Eleanor thoughtfully, "that the Henry in the poem is Uncle Freddy's Henry? Thoreau did live in Walden woods!"

"Or maybe it's some Henry in the Bible," said Edward. "See? It talks about the Garden of Eden."

"Where's Coromandel?" said Eleanor.

"Some place in China?" hazarded Edward.

"Did Uncle Freddy's Henry play the flute?" said Eleanor.

Eddy didn't know. Eleanor decided to ask Uncle Freddy. She found him in the parlor. He was washing Henry's face. "Now, old fellow," said Uncle Freddy, "just be patient while I scrub behind your ears. There! Now for a good wipe!" Henry disappeared behind a huge Turkish towel, vigorously handled by Uncle Freddy, and emerged again looking clean and white.

Eleanor looked at his calm marble face. "Did he play the flute, Uncle Freddy?" she said. "Did he hoe beans? Did he wear an old suit?"

"Who, Henry?" said Uncle Freddy. "Of course he does!"

That settled it! For once they had figured out a clue cleverly and correctly! Eleanor and Edward went into an excited whispered conference. They agreed that Henry must have been a rich hermit, who had buried diamonds and pearls under his cabin on the shore of Walden Pond. Perhaps they were still there! Hastily they gathered shovels for digging, and an old gladstone bag to carry the jewels back home in.

Aunt Lily wanted to know what they were up to. "Just a hike down to Walden Pond," said Edward.

The shovels had to be explained. Eleanor thought quickly. "To collect rocks," she said.

Then Uncle Freddy wanted to go, too. "I'll just pay a call on Henry," he said.

Eleanor and Edward looked at each other in dismay, but Aunt Lily asked them to take him along. "It will be a nice outing for him, poor dear," she said.

They started off, an odd threesome, walking down the road. On the other side of the turnpike they came upon some boys who had hitchhiked out from Boston, their towels tucked into their belts. Uncle Freddy made them a speech. "My friends," he shouted, "Walden is as sacred as the Ganges! It is a gem of the first water which Concord wears in her coronet!" Edward and Eleanor were terribly embarrassed, and they tugged at Uncle Freddy.

But he wouldn't stop. The boys nudged one another, and began to run. Uncle Freddy pulled away from Edward and sprinted along the center of the road. Cars full of bathers honked at him, and their drivers leaned out to shout.

But Uncle Freddy neither saw nor heard. The boys he had been chasing soon outdistanced him. He didn't care. He was returning, at last, to Henry's Walden, that quiet pond where one man had sought a refuge from village life, and had stayed to be self-appointed inspector of snowstorms and rainstorms, and to hear with his own ears what was written on the wind.

Suddenly Uncle Freddy veered his course and plunged into the woods. Edward and Eleanor were glad to leave the main road. They followed him clumsily as he danced along the woodland path. "Henry's house should be right in here somewhere," he said. They came upon several other people—a tall young man who had his arm around a girl, and an old man sleeping with a newspaper over his face. "So many to pay their respects to Henry today!" rejoiced Uncle Freddy.

Then all at once they came to a cleared area. There was a pile of stones there, and a square of ground marked off with chains. There were more stones half-buried in the ground. One of them had an inscription. Edward read it aloud—

BENEATH THESE STONES
LIES THE CHIMNEY FOUNDATION
OF THOREAU'S CABIN 1845-1847

Eleanor looked at Uncle Freddy. What would he say? Uncle Freddy stared at the stone. Then he bent over it and read it to himself. "Well!" he said, "he's not at home." He stood up shakily. "I'll call another day," he said. Then Uncle Freddy shambled off, blinking, and wandered sadly along the shore of the pond.

Eleanor suddenly felt overcome by the melancholy of the late summer day and the dusty untidy woods. She sat down on one of the chains and pushed herself idly back and forth. Edward looked doubtfully at the pile of stones. It was almost as high as he was. If there were Brazilian diamonds and pearls from Coromandel anywhere here, they were buried under the stones. Tentatively he toyed with his spade. Where should they start? Should they move all the stones?

They were aroused by a shout from Uncle Freddy. For a foolish moment they wondered if he had found the treasure. They stumbled down the path to the shore and ran along the edge of the water, looking for him. They found him staring across at the opposite side of the pond, where the public bathing beach was, and waving his arms. It had finally dawned on Uncle Freddy that the swarms of bathers there had not come to Walden to pay their respects to Henry Thoreau.

"Who dares to defile this gem in Concord's crown?" he cried. Then he was off again, running around the shore to the beach, ranting and shouting and waving his hat. Edward and Eleanor lunged after him. Oh, why had they come? The spades bounced uncomfortably on Eddy's shoulder, and Eleanor suddenly felt absurd with the big gladstone bag. To think that they had expected to fill its bulging old sides with pearls!

"Oh, Uncle Freddy," cried Eleanor, "please stop and let's go home!"

But Uncle Freddy wouldn't stop. He was romping ankle-deep in the water now, soaking his shoes and his baggy knickers to the knees. He shouted at the bathers, and made so much noise that he almost drowned out the happy screams of small boys jumping off the dock. He scooped up some water with his hands and splashed it at an elderly lady bather, who fell back in the water and had to be rescued by her husband. The husband turned out to be Mr. Preek, looking astonishing in a voluminous striped suit. Furious, Mr. Preek started splashing Uncle

Freddy back. There was a violent white-water battle. Uncle Freddy was soon wet all over.

But he seemed to exult in being drenched. "Tell me, brother, what are we?" he bellowed at Mr. Preek. "Spirits, bathing in the sea of Deity!" Then, suddenly, he abandoned that encounter and waded sloppily to the dock. He climbed on and charged along it, leaping nimbly over prostrate sunbathers. He galloped right to the deep end and plunged off it headfirst. He was aiming a watery attack on an old fellow who was floating peacefully along in a rubber inner tube.

"He'll drown," cried Eleanor desperately. She ran after him, but she was caught in a milling tide of curious bathers. She slipped on the wet dock and was almost trampled on. Edward burrowed between them and was just in time to see Uncle Freddy being hauled out by an angry lifeguard. As soon as he was back on his feet, wheezing and blowing, Uncle Freddy slipped loose and took off again. He rushed at the crowd, clapping his hands, the water in his knickers ballooning them out around his knees.

"Get along!" he cried. "Get along home!" He chased a shrieking, laughing band of hulking boys and girls off the dock. Then they ambushed him and counterattacked with towels and huge striped rubber balls. An inner tube ringed Uncle Freddy neatly, pinning his arms to his sides. He sprinted away, struggling with it. They chased him all the way up the steep concrete steps to the street, the brawny lifeguard in the lead and Mr. Preek gasping in the rear. Edward and Eleanor, abandoning their possessions, chased him, too. What, oh, what would Aunt Lily say?

Astonishingly, Uncle Freddy stayed out in front. He surged past the trailer park and put on speed. His pursuers would never have caught him at all, if he hadn't suddenly swerved and rushed at a hot-dog stand, and thrown himself at the wavy surface of a comic mirror that was fastened to the outside. His own distorted image had become the enemy. "G-grease-spot!" he howled, with chattering teeth, recoiling and hurling himself at it again. "Horny-handed h-harpy on the shore of the Icarian S-sea!"

The lifeguard got to him first and handled him roughly, then the crowd of laughing bathers and Mr. Preek, and at last the police. They had been summoned by the hot-dog man, who didn't understand enough of Uncle Freddy's remarks to be insulted but recognized an escaping lunatic when he saw one.

Edward and Eleanor caught up just in time to see Uncle Freddy bundled into a car, handcuffed to a policeman. They struggled home, climbed sobbing up the steps, and broke the news to Aunt Lily.

She clasped her hands. "It was my fault," she said. "I should never have let him go." She bustled around for clean warm clothes for Uncle Freddy. Then she climbed into her car and drove with grim courage to the Town Hall. Uncle Freddy had been taken there and thrust, dripping, behind bars. Aunt Lily talked sensibly to the police chief and he finally agreed to discharge Uncle Freddy in her care.

But they had a hard time getting him to leave his cell. He wanted to stay, and he hung onto the bars with all his might. "H-Henry spent a whole night in j-jail," he cried, "and s-so will I!" But finally, with gentle talk and soft words, Aunt Lily persuaded him to come home.

Mr. Preek came along, with a piece of paper for Aunt Lily to sign. It said that Uncle Freddy should be locked up in an asylum where he couldn't do any harm, or come to any. But Aunt Lily burst into tears and refused to sign it. Mr. Preek left, with harsh words.

Edward and Eleanor, thoroughly exhausted, went to bed early. They were almost too tired to climb the three sets of stairs to the tower room. Eleanor, lying in bed and drifting off to sleep, thought once again about the diamonds and pearls. Were the jewels really buried at Walden? And if so, where? Should they dig under the pile of stones? Or elsewhere? Drowsily she imagined them hiring a ship and sailing to Brazil, or floating lazily in an inner tube all the way to Coromandel, wherever that might be.

II

PEARLS FROM COROMANDEL, DIAMONDS FROM BRAZIL

*E*LEANOR FELT SMALL, terribly small, much smaller than she had ever felt before. Her small heart was beating at great speed. She was furry. Her arms were crouched under her, and they had a new kind of wiry, tiny strength. Her ears felt strangely different, and huge, and alive to different sorts of whisperings and cracklings and rustlings. At the end of her nose was a strange sensation, a kind of trembling awareness. She reached up a hand and felt at her nose. The fingers of the hand wouldn't separate. They were attached together and folded into a smooth little paw, but they could feel long vibrating hairs fanning out into—whiskers! Behind her was another strange thing—a sense of sensitive support at the rear, a long agile prop—a tail! She was a mouse!

Her whisker ends brushed something nearby. It felt warm and friendly and furry. Eleanor crowded closer and snuggled against it, fur against fur. It was another mouse. "Hello," said Edward. "Isn't this nice?"

"Where are we?" said Eleanor, looking up. Her eyes felt big and beady and sharp. Her nose quivered and wrinkled. There was a new kind of cleverness in her five senses, and another kind of sixth sense that seemed instinct in every smooth hair of her coat, and all down the bare length of her tail to the very tip.

"I think this is a nest," said Edward.

"I think it's *our* nest," said Eleanor. Through a hole in the top of the nest she could see the night sky. She made a sudden movement and found herself looking out of the hole. Eddy silked his way up beside her. It was wonderful to move like a mouse! Together they looked out. Their nest lay in the forked branch of an alder that stood among other alders at the edge of a body of water. "Is it the ocean?" said Eleanor.

Edward studied it a minute. "No," he said, "it's Walden Pond. Come on. I want to feel what it's like to run with four feet."

The two mice crept out of their nest, their heads cocked and alert. Then, swiftly, they ran down to the ground and darted into the leafy cover of the shore.

Running on four feet, Edward decided joyfully, was more like roller-skating than anything else. His four legs worked rhythmically and knowingly under him, with a thousand rapid patterings, and the rest of him was carried along smoothly, without the bumps and jogs and sharp recoil that lumbering human feet make when they hit the hard ground. He wanted to try it some more. "Let's go," he said. He poked his wriggling nose out from under the enormous umbrella of a dried oak leaf and then scurried forth on his roller-skate feet again.

Eleanor followed, with a few nervous half-starts. Why did it seem so natural to cower under the leaf, and to rush so quickly from one cover to the next? Timidly she darted after Eddy, who was scrambling happily from one great pebble along the shore to another. "Come on," she said, "let's look for Ned and Nora."

Eddy pattered on ahead. "Where do you think we should look?" he said, poking his nose this way and that under the growth along the shore. He was trying to find a clear lane along which he could try to get up some real speed. At last he found what he was looking for. Under the tree-like growth of the blueberry bushes and the sumach there were little branching paths, minute little highways along which he could scuttle at breakneck speed, his reluctant mouse-sister hurrying after him.

Intersecting these tiny hidden byways were broader avenues. Whose thoroughfares were these? They soon found out.

"Look out!" warned Eleanor, nipping Edward's tail. Her teeth were wonderfully sharp, and Edward was hurt so badly he leaped sideways. But he was just in time to be out of the way of the vast hairy body that came lumbering down the right-of-way. The two mice cowered under a clump of fern that was like a forest of palm trees, and watched it go by. It was a raccoon, padding on his four black hands along the path on the way to the water's edge to paddle in the shallows.

"Let's just stay here and watch the world go by," said Eleanor. They made themselves comfortable between the bristling stumps of long-dead ferns and looked out with their bright black eyes. Their mouse-hearts fluttered, and their marvelous ears cocked this way and that, picking up earfuls of news. They heard a loon's weird cry in the water—now near, now far away. Something in Eleanor's velvet hide told her that she was safe. She leaned against Edward, enjoying his brotherly warmth, and savoring the sense of being nothing at all, a part of the night and of the woods and nothing more. There was a goose honking over the pond, and high above them in the top of a hickory tree the sound of a wood thrush singing. "Listen, listen," said Edward.

Then there was another sound. Edward and Eleanor were aware of it at the same instant and cocked their ears toward it. It was a deep, earth-shaking double thud. There was nothing animal-like or bird-like about it. It was a solid, rhythmical, steady boom-boom, as of a great weight driving into the ground. It approached and grew stronger. Then it cast a giant shadow across the moon, and the two little mice looked up and up. It was a man.

He was walking along the forest path, his knees brushing against the blueberry bushes, his boots treading softly, heel-toe, heel-toe, but carrying such height and weight in them that they sent solid vibrations into the ground.

"Let's follow him," said Eddy. They crept out of the protection of the clump of fern and ran after him in little rushes to this side and that. Where was he going?

He was going home. And home was a little house in the middle of the woods, growing up like something as natural to the woods as the pitch pines creaking against its shingles. The thudding stopped. The towering man stood still. He was reaching into his pocket. Then he stooped and sprinkled something on the ground. Edward and Eleanor stopped in their tracks and watched. But the man didn't look at them. Instead he got up again to his full height and disappeared against the

91

blackness of the house. They could hear his door open and shut, and a moment later they could see light shining through the small panes of glass in the window. He was gone.

Edward discovered at the end of his wrinkling nose a tremendous curiosity. What had the man scattered on the ground? He moved cautiously forward, his nose leading the way surely and certainly. Ah, here it was. He had found a large bread crumb. He gobbled it, then found another and took it back to Eleanor. She had never seen anything that looked or smelled so delicious. She sat up on her hind legs, held the bread crumb between her front paws, and ate it delicately.

She wanted another. Edward was already out again, foraging. He came back. "Come on," he said, "get your own. There's hundreds of them! He put them there just for us."

Eleanor ran her tongue over her mouse-chops. Never in her girl-life had she tasted anything so good as that bread crumb. But the clearing where the crumbs were scattered was empty of cover. Eleanor peered out into the moonlight, sought out a single tempting bread crumb, scampered out after it, picked it up with her teeth, and hurried back. Then she reared up comfortably again and ate it between her paws. Goodness, but it was satisfying! It tasted like more.

And more tasted like still more. Eleanor picked up one crumb at a time, then two. Edward was simply wandering from crumb to tempting crumb. Just one more, he kept saying to himself, then he would run back under the leaves. There was a particularly delicious-looking piece of crust over there. He started for it. But Eleanor was there first. She bit deeply into it, and started to eat it there and then. Edward batted at her with his paw. "I saw it first," he said.

"Finders, keepers," squeaked Eleanor sharply. She gnawed daintily away. Edward angrily sank his long teeth into the other end of the crust and tugged. For a moment the two of them jerked feverishly at it, glaring into each other's eyes. They were so enraged with one another that they paid no attention to a new sound—a soft rushing whirring overhead.

All at once the bread gave way. And as Eleanor fell over, every hair on her body stood on end. "BEWARE!" cried her sixth sense. There was a huge dark shape above her, grasping and grasping. If the bread hadn't broken, the shape would have had her. She leaped to her feet and darted this way and that way, in tacking fits and starts. The shadow disappeared, then fell on her again. It missed, then it lifted and hovered over her. Eleanor skittered frantically from side to side, her rapid mouse heartbeat accelerated to a terrible staccato thumping.

But suddenly Eddy was ahead of her, running. He squeaked at her, "To the house! Hole in the cellar!" Then he spurted away, leading the great looming, flopping, grasping shadow after him. Eleanor made a dash for the house, scrambled over the stones of the foundation, found a chink between them, and tumbled in. Then she scrabbled back to the hole and looked out.

It was an owl, an ordinary New England screech owl. Eddy was running spasmodically in short left-right-left dashes in front of it, but each dash was a little shorter, and with each one the owl missed him by less and less of a hairsbreadth. They were coming this way. Could he reach the side of the house and safety? "Come on, Eddy!" squealed Eleanor. He was almost there. But the owl was there first. It flopped between Eddy and the house. Eddy stopped short. The great owl-eyes glowed at him. Hypnotized, Eddy stared back. It was very odd, but it was true—he recognized the owl. The face of the bird of prey, with its shadowed eyes and hooked beak, was one he had seen before. Wasn't it the same as—? But the owl was lifting its talons to plunge at him.

Then Eleanor helped. With a mighty shove, with all her miniature strength, she dislodged a loose pebble from the side of the hole in the wall. It fell on the owl's back, and the bird flapped a few feet into the air, with a disconcerted screech. Not far, but just far enough for

Eddy to see his chance and take it. Breathlessly, just ahead of the owl's claws, he tumbled into the dark opening in the wall and lay panting on his side on the floor.

Eleanor huddled against him and waited. She could feel Eddy's sides heaving up and down. After a while the heaving stopped, but he lay still a moment longer. At last he was recovered enough to stand up on his four feet. They were ready to look about them. And ready to listen to something besides the hammering of their own hearts. Why, there was music! From far overhead, floating down through the cracks in the floorboards, there came a thin reedy fluting. The notes wandered mournfully up and down. They made no recognizable melody. They sounded more like the natural music of the loon or the wood thrush out-of-doors than any man-made music.

Edward and Eleanor had to see for themselves. They ran up a pile of sacks smoothly rounded with grain and found a knothole in one of the floorboards. They squeezed through it and scuttled across the floor of the lighted room to a hiding place beside the hearth. From there they could look out and observe the man.

He sat turned away from them, at a small table, leaning his chair back on its two rear legs. He was blowing on a wooden flute. The haunting music charmed them. They had but one thought—to see his face. Carefully they crept out of their hiding place, and moved noise-lessly around the wall to the other side of the small room. From here they could see only the thick trousers and the heavy boots.

Then the music stopped, and the chair tipped for-ward onto all four legs. The flute was put down, there was a rustling of paper, and then there began a strange scratching noise. What was he doing? The two mice simply had to know. Softly they ran up one of the rear legs of his table, and hid behind a pair of books that lay on its top. From there they could peer out cautiously at him.

The scratching sound had come from his pen. He was writing. "It's Henry," whispered Eleanor.

It was Henry, indeed. He was homelier than the sculptured Henry that stood in their parlor at home, but his face had a kind of sun-browned strength. He was looking down at the page across which his pen was moving so surely.

Edward's beady eyes looked down at it, too. And there he saw something extraordinary. "Oh, Eleanor, look!" he said, pointing at it with his paw. Then she saw it, too. Out of Henry's scratching pen a series of shining blots was flowing. They were jewels. They lay upon the paper like sentences of pearls, whole paragraphs and pages of glittering diamonds. It was the treasure they had been seeking, the pearls from Coromandel, the diamonds from Brazil.

And having found the treasure, Eleanor and Edward came to the end of their dream, and burrowed their way back into consciousness in the real world of the morning. They woke up together, and sat up in their beds. Someone was calling.

It was Aunt Lily, hallooing up the attic stairs. "Hurry up, children!" she was saying. "It's the first day of school!"

Edward got up first, feeling unpleasantly pink and smooth without his mousy fur, and clumsily gigantesque. He rubbed the places where his whiskers had been. "No more roller-skating," he said sadly.

Eleanor was leaning up on one elbow, thinking. "The treasure was in the book he was writing. What book was it?"

"It was *Walden*," said Eddy promptly. "He lived at Walden Pond and kept a journal, and then he wrote it all over again later and called the book *Walden*." (Not for nothing was Edward the nephew of Uncle Freddy.) "I'll bet we'll find the jewels in the book, with the pages pasted together and the inside hollowed out like a box!" He ran to the bookcase. "Aha!" he said, "here it is!" He pulled out a book and flopped it open.

How disappointing! The pages all riffled separately

apart. There was nothing on them or in them but black print. Disgusted, Eddy threw the book on the floor.

Eleanor got up and squatted down beside it. She picked it up and looked at the outside. It was *Walden*, all right, by Henry David Thoreau. She opened it, and the book fell open at the flyleaf. And here Eleanor found the "jewels." Written there were these words, in a familiar script:

To Ned and Nora. Here are Henry's jewels—his Walden, a treasure for the world beyond price. I hope when you are grown-up you will read it, and see that its words are what Henry hoped they were: "pearls from Coromandel and diamonds from Brazil"! From your affectionate friend, Krishna.

Now, wasn't that just like a grown-up! The treasure was a book! The diamonds and pearls were just words, words anybody could have for the reading! Edward grabbed the book. He meant to throw it at the wall! Then something made him stop. He looked at it, then put it carefully back in the bookcase. He put on his bathrobe and went whistling down the ladder-steps. "Someday I'll have to read it," he said, as his head disappeared below the trap door.

Eleanor watched the top of his red head go down.

Then she remembered something and shuddered. Part of the dream had been a nightmare. They might have been killed! And the treasure had hardly been worth the danger! Would all the others be like that? An old music box, a broken doll, an old book? Surely some of the others would be exchangeable for cold, hard cash?

12

MIRROR, MIRROR
ON THE WALL

*E*DWARD STOOD SPREAD-LEGGED, his empty lunchbox in one hand, an after-school licorice stick dangling from his mouth, and peered into the perfect silver surface of the gazing globe in the front yard. With his nose next to it his reflection looked like some strange kind of creature with a giant proboscis and a small pinhead. His hand, sticky from the licorice, made black smudges on the ball. The huge wooden house behind him was reflected in miniature, its walls bulging with the curve, its towers shrinking backward.

It had occurred to Edward that the gazing globe might be the mirror mentioned in the mystic verse. "O crystal ball," he said, "what do my tomorrows hold?"

The gazing globe was silent. No miraculous picture bloomed up in the reflection. Edward asked it where the treasure was, and Ned and Nora and Prince Krishna. Nothing happened. Then he asked it if Edward Hall would ever be President of the United States. "Tell me, O crystal ball!" he said.

Just for a moment he thought something was happening in the gazing globe. A small spidery form detached itself from the background and became larger and larger. Suddenly it was his sister's spectacled face, looking enormously back at him. Edward crossed his eyes at her and stuck out his tongue, which was a horrible black from the licorice.

"Look out," said Eleanor cheerfully, "your face might freeze that way!" Then she gave a little cry. "Oh, look at my nose!"

"It isn't really that big," said Edward.

"I know, but my freckles, I've got more!" Eleanor covered her nose with her hand, aghast. "Please, oh, please, crystal ball," she said, "tell me it isn't true!" She made mystic motions with her hands over the ball. Then she jumped. Something had suddenly started up in the reflection and nearly filled it—a monstrous head with ginger hair. It was Uncle Freddy.

"Oh, Uncle Freddy," said Eleanor, "just look at my new freckles! I've got more, haven't I? Be honest! I do, don't I?" She stood up and looked at him, her forehead wrinkled, her new-found freckles displayed with shining frankness in the Indian-summer sunshine.

Uncle Freddy looked down at her and smiled. "My little tiger lily," he said. "Faces of children are like flowers, a bit of natural beauty." He chucked Eleanor fondly under the chin, and then his expression changed. "But faces of grown-ups are man-made! There's never an instant's truce between virtue and vice! Beware how you paint yourself!"

"Paint?" said Eleanor, thinking hopefully of powder and rouge. "Do you think paint would cover them up?"

"No, no," said Uncle Freddy, turning vaguely away. "I meant what Henry said—that we are all sculptors and painters, and our material is our own flesh and blood and bones." He turned back and shook his finger at her. "So carve yourself well!" Then he stooped and looked at his own odd face in the gazing globe. There, of course, it looked odder still. "Ah, well," he said, and all at once there were tears in his eyes, "it's what we could have been that breaks the heart—there is no limit to our capacity!" He flung out his arms in a grand, generous gesture, and shouted a glorious question of his friend Waldo's: "Who can set bounds to the possibilities of a man?"

Eleanor and Edward listened respectfully. Were they supposed to answer? But Uncle Freddy dropped his arms, rubbed his sleeve over his eyes, and went away. He was mumbling a phrase, over and over—"private infinitude, private infinitude!"

Aunt Lily, who was sandwiching fall house cleaning in between her piano pupils, stood on the porch with her sleeves rolled up, energetically shaking out a dust-mop. Something Uncle Freddy had said reminded her of her favorite hymn, by James Russell Lowell, and now she brandished her dust-mop in time and started to sing it in her strong clear contralto:

> *Once to every man and nation*
> *Comes the moment to decide,*
> *In the strife of truth with falsehood,*
> *For the good or evil side . . .*

The hymn had a threatening gloom that she loved—dust kitties flew rhythmically out over the sprawling forsythia bushes, and Aunt Lily sang on, as direfully as she could, the solemn last words of the first verse:

> *And the choice goes by forever*
> *Twixt that darkness and that light!*

"Put down your mop, Aunt Lily," said Edward, "here comes a broom!"

It was a broom—Mary Jane Broom, marching up the walk, all ready to torture her teacher with a new lesson, perfect note for note, hideous in noise. Aunt Lily sighed, put down her mop, and assumed her pleasant teacher-manner.

Eleanor stared at Mary Jane. She was Miss Prawn's niece, and her complexion was as white and pink as a good little girl's could be. Eleanor felt rebellious. All the rest of the day she kept running her fingers over the bridge of her nose. She couldn't feel her freckles, but she knew that they were there. She was still worrying about them as she lay in bed.

The light was out, and Edward had already gone to sleep. Eleanor hunched herself up under the covers and sat with her long red hair streaming over her knees, staring across the room into the mirror that rose up on the gigantic old dresser. She could just see herself, a silhouette humped up in bed. She asked the mirror a question—

Mirror, mirror on the wall,
What's to become of Eleanor Hall?

Who would ever marry anybody who was skinny and wore glasses and had freckles all over her face? Certainly not Benjamin Parks! Eleanor would have to be an old maid, like Aunt Lily, and give piano lessons. Or maybe she would be a nurse, or a teacher. Who or what was she to be, one day? Eleanor felt sorry for her pitiful self, and a tear fell on her pillow. She went to sleep at last, but not until she had made up her mind about something. Tomorrow morning she was going to borrow some of the face powder on Aunt Lily's dressing table and cover her freckles with it. Aunt Lily didn't use it herself, and she'd never miss it.

Then, as Eleanor and Edward slept, the full October moon rose clear and sailed up into the sky. Its light passed through the stone in the middle of the window and travelled across the room to the great dark world of the mirror. From there it was reflected back to the window again, to hit squarely one sloping triangular facet of the stone and be returned at a minute angle. From the mirror once more it made a journey at the speed of light to another facet of the stone, a long rectangular cleavage that instantly turned it back upon itself. Over and over again the reflecting surfaces of the stone returned the light to the mirror. Over and over again the mirror sent its rays back, until, infinity folded upon infinity, the reflections were beyond counting.

13

THE GIFT OF THE MIRROR

*T*HEY WERE VERY SMALL. They were walking across a marble plain. It was the dresser top. Ned and Nora were walking ahead of them, not far away. It was dark, but Eleanor could see them dimly, and she could hear them talking. Ned had his arm up now, pointing at something. "Catch them!" said Edward. They started to run.

Then Ned and Nora were gone. Eleanor stopped. Where were they? Eddy looked up at the big mirror-frame. Had they climbed up to the shelves? If only he had brought a rope and some climbing spikes! Trebor Nosnibor would never be without a rope! He would carry one always, attached to his belt, right next to his beautiful jackknife with its six or seven different blades. Edward stood beside the mirror-frame and felt idly around it for handholds.

Eleanor had no intention of climbing anything. She was fascinated instead by the dark vastness of the mirror. What would a tiny creature like herself look like in so monstrous a field of glass? She walked slowly toward it. The mirror was completely dark. Then all at once she blundered into the path of the moonlight, as it poured back and forth upon itself from the window. The whole great length of the window was suddenly flooded with light.

"Eddy, Eddy," shrieked Eleanor, "look, look!" By dint of some shifting back and forth, Eddy managed to stand in the same relation to the light-path. Together they looked at their reflections in the mirror.

It was like a mirror he had seen once, Eddy decided, a double mirror, that had reflected him over and over and on and on, into a dim infinity. Here he was again, a thousand times over, a million times over, a million-million times! This mirror was much clearer than the other. All the Edwards were sharp and crystalline, the thousandth one as clear as the first, only a little rainbow-colored from the multiplicity of the reflection. If he lifted his right hand, half of the Edwards lifted their right hands, and all the rest lifted their left. He danced a jig. The million Edwards danced, too.

And Eleanor saw the same Eleanor over and over again, each strand of her red hair, each freckle, infinitely and perfectly repeated. The reflections were so perfect that it was almost as though there were no hard dividing glass in front of them at all. She walked forward and reached out her hand to touch it. It should be about here. But it was not. She crept forward again, pushing her feet ahead of her carefully, expecting to be brought up against an invisible wall. It must be right about here somewhere! She couldn't have passed it?

Eleanor looked back. Why, there was the crack in the marble that meant the end of the real dresser top and the beginning of the reflected one—and it was *behind* her! She whirled around. Where was Eddy? He had gone through, too! Eleanor turned again and felt with her hands at the place where the *back* surface of the mirror should have been. It was all soft, black, impalpable air—the enormous frame rising up on either side and melting with the blackness of the night. Doubtfully she looked again into the depths of the mirror-world.

Before them stretched the million Eleanors, the million Edwards—sparkling, brilliant, each in a glassy shaft of reflected light. The real Eleanor leaned over to her brother. The millions of reflected Eleanors leaned over, too. The real Eleanor whispered in the real Edward's ear, "Ned and Nora must have come into the mirror." The millions of reflected Eleanors whispered, and the sound of their whispering was like a great sh-sh-shushing. Eleanor straightened up. So did all the others. The whispering sound gradually became fainter and finally stopped.

"It's just an echo," decided Edward. "They didn't really say anything."

"Come on," said Eleanor, "let's see if we can find Ned and Nora."

They walked forward. It was like walking into a maze of mirrors. If you walked fearlessly straight ahead, you found yourself within the next mirror and approaching two others. You could choose either one, then go through that one to two more; choose one of those, and find two more. It was as though they stood at this moment at the apex of an infinite choice. But once they chose, they would have to stick to that part of the maze, and the further they went in, the harder it would be to go back. Which way had Ned and Nora gone?

Edward studied the first two reflected Edwards. Were they exactly alike? Or was there something a little different in the expression of the left-hand one, something ever so slightly disagreeable about the curve of the mouth? "That's the way you look when you're being stubborn," said Eleanor, chuckling and pointing to it.

There were two Eleanors, too, to choose between. One of them stood beside the slightly stubborn-looking Edward. That one looked a little paler than the other. Why? Eleanor remembered that she had decided to powder her freckles; now she could see a distinct chalky blotch on the nose. She looked at the other one. It had the usual complement of freckles, the same ordinary Eleanor-look.

Eleanor prodded Edward. "Let's try that one," she said, and, grabbing his hand, she pulled him into the left-hand mirror, the one with the stubborn-looking Edward and the pale-looking Eleanor.

"No," said Edward, "wait!" But it was too late. They were inside. "I thought I caught a glimpse of Ned and Nora, just then, in the other mirror," he said crossly.

"You did?" said Eleanor. She felt a little uneasy. She, too, had caught a glimpse of something as she passed through the mirror threshold, but it was within *this* mirror that she had seen it—just a momentary flash—a glimpse of a face, grinning at her and beckoning. Was she foolish to think she had seen it, or was it really the Jack-in-the-box?

"Look," said Edward, "they're stiff now, like statues."

Their images were still there. They hadn't disappeared when Eleanor and Eddy stepped across the mirror-sill, but they no longer imitated them. They just stood motionless. They were absolutely perfect copies of the real Eleanor and the real Edward. Nose for nose, ear for ear, eyelash for eyelash, cowlick for cowlick, Edward's reflection was like Edward—and there was just the merest hint of a stubborn look about the mouth. Edward stood in front of it and made the same look with his own. "You're frozen that way, now," said Eleanor.

Shyly, then, she looked at her own image, and reached out a hand to touch its face. It was as soft and warm as her real face. She patted the powder on its nose, then smoothed it to either side a little, to blend it in. As she did so, some of the freckles underneath began to show through again. "Oh, dear," said Eleanor, "I wish I had a little more powder." She looked around.

There was no powder to be had. But there was another pair of Edwards and Eleanors. She looked quickly at the two new Eleanors. One of them had a shiny, washed-looking nose, but the other looked as though she had found the powder box. And there was a little wrinkle between the eyebrows of this Eleanor that looked rather—what? Discontented? Worldly-wise?

Without even looking at the two Edwards, Eleanor dragged her brother after her into the side of the mirror where the freckleless Eleanor stood. Edward protested. They began to argue. The argument became a scuffle, then a fight. They began yanking and dragging and tugging one another into new openings of the mirror-maze. Sometimes Edward won, sometimes Eleanor. They stopped looking at the images, and just lurched and shoved each other among them. Then all at once Edward stopped fighting and looked at the frozen statue of himself into which he had tumbled.

Like all the rest it was brightly lit. He was looking at the back of it. There was something odd about the neck. Eleanor stared at it, too. Slowly they walked around to the front, and looked at it in horror.

It was Edward, all right. But an older Edward, a middle-aged Edward, a dreadful Edward. The stubborn expression that had been boyish and soft about the mouth of the first Edward was cast now into a grim tightness, a rock-hard bluish line. The eyes were shadowed and dark and lifeless, and the whole face was seamed with ruthless, ugly lines.

"I don't like it," cried Edward. He touched it. It was as warm and real as the first. Then he gave his sister a frightened glance, and together they turned to look at the Eleanor that matched this version of Edward.

Eleanor took one look and covered her mouth with her hands. Her image was worse than Edward's, worse! "Oh, no, no!" screamed Eleanor, and turned to escape. "Choose, choose!" she said, "oh, let's be careful how we choose!" Together they stared at the next pair of images.

But there was no choice. There was only one more set—one Edward, one Eleanor—a frightening, savage Edward, and a terrible, tawdry Eleanor.

They turned this way and that, looking for the other pair of images. But there were no more. They had come so far in the wrong direction that they could no longer choose at all. They could go only one way. The choices had shrivelled down to one alone, and that was no better than none at all.

Or could they go back? They hadn't tried that yet. And when they did, the lights went out. All was in blackness. They groped behind them in the dark. Would the mirrors be frozen up behind them, walling them in? That wouldn't be fair! After all, it was only a dream, only a kind of game! They hadn't really lived this awful life yet and made themselves into these dreadful creatures!

Made themselves! That was what Uncle Freddy had said, thought Eleanor. "Beware how you paint yourself! Carve yourself well!" She collided painfully with Edward. Then they held hands and struggled on in the total darkness. For what seemed like hours, they battled their way backwards through the maze, feeling for the path by which they had come. They were continually running up against mirror walls and striking against their own images. Sometimes they took wrong turnings altogether and wandered so far off the main track that they almost gave up hope of ever finding it again. At last one of the images, after giving Edward a dreadful crack across the shoulder when he blundered into it, proved to be one that he remembered. It was one of the smaller ones, and he had been hit by the baseball bat in its hands. Eddy reached up and felt for the top of its head. "It's only about a half-inch taller than me," he said.

There began to be a little light. At first it was more confusing than helpful, feebly reflected by the complexity of the mirrored surfaces. But soon they were able to interpret true image from false and find their way with only an occasional wrong turning.

At last Eleanor recognized the back of the first of the reflected Eleanors, the one with the faint dusting of powder on its nose. "Hateful girl," she said.

Then they stood outside the mirror-maze, looking back at it. Again all the multitudinous images were visible in bright light, again they could look at the original pairs. Should they choose once more?

"You said Ned and Nora went that way?" said Eleanor, pointing at the mirror image of Edward that looked bland and friendly in the usual way.

"Yes," said Edward. They stepped through the

mirror into the right-hand side. And then they stepped through into the next. The choosing was easy, when they looked a little carefully.

The statue-like images were getting taller. Eleanor decided to concentrate on the reflections of Edward. There was no denying that they were getting very good-looking. One of the Edwards they chose had a gay red mustache and chin-whiskers that made them laugh. But the next Edward seemed to have shaved them off. After a while the real Eleanor and the real Edward became quite shy. Their elder selves overawed them. Edward's grew as tall as Eleanor's, and then taller. His plumpness was gone. He had grown to a strong, stocky middle height. Eleanor's images grew willowy and slender.

They stopped for a moment and walked around their images, not saying anything. "I don't suppose we'll ever be as nice as that," faltered Eleanor.

"No," said Edward. "You've still got freckles, I see, though," he said.

There were freckles there, all right, hardly faded at all. Eleanor could see that they didn't matter. "I like them," she said stoutly.

"Now what?" said Edward, turning to the mirror-maze again.

"Look what's happened!" said Eleanor.

Instead of two choices, there were many. They were unable to choose which was the best, so they picked one at random. And beyond that choice lay a hundred, and beyond the next a thousand. Just as the other maze had led them down a narrowing path until there was no choice left, this one opened out into wide and shining worlds of possibility.

Eleanor and Edward wandered up and down, looking at the images of themselves, overwhelmed by what they saw. One of the Eleanors was an artist. They watched her brush a wild streak of red across a canvas, then stand back and stare at it, biting her lip. Another was a teacher, standing in front of a blackboard. A third Eleanor seemed to be a writer of some kind, possibly a poet, because she was sitting at a table frowning at the words RHYMING DICTIONARY on the jacket of a book, and opening it and riffling through the pages. Another was obviously a doctor. She was wearing a white coat and peering into a small boy's ear.

Edward's were all sorts of things, too. There were scientists of various kinds, and a mathematician, and a professor with chalk dust all over his coat. Edward looked at all of these, then stopped suddenly in front of the next.

This one was very dashing! It was dressed in a kind of romantic, swashbuckling way, with high leather boots and short trousers and a pith helmet. There were all sorts of useful tools hanging on its belt, including a complicated jackknife that simply sprouted blades.

Edward could see all the blades quite clearly. There were three ordinary knife blades, a screwdriver blade, a can opener, a saw, a leather punch, and a corkscrew. There was even an infinitesimal pair of scissors. What a magnificent tool! Who or what was this image supposed to be? Then Edward spotted the coil of rope dangling neatly from its belt, and he knew. It was none other than Trebor Nosnibor!

And next to Trebor was another odd one. Edward couldn't make it out. It was sitting at a big desk, studying a pile of papers. Edward stopped over and looked up at the face. There was something about it that he liked— but what? The red hair was receding a little bit from its brow, and the eyes, concentrating on the papers before them, had a determined, courageous look.

Edward stood up again. He didn't know which of them to choose.

Eleanor didn't wait to think. Instantly she chose the mysterious image of herself, the one that might or might not be a poet. But then as the poetical mirror opened wide, she had to put her hands over her ears. Behind the chosen Eleanor three noisy little boys were jumping on a sofa. A baby girl lay in a buggy. The buggy trembled as the baby shook her tiny fists and howled. Children! Eleanor laughed. She could be a poet and a mother at the same time. She poked her brother and said, "Look, Eddy, look."

But it was the tall poetry-writing Eleanor who answered. "Thank you," she murmured, leaning over the table and scribbling something, "a rhyme for boathook." Then she pushed back her chair and picked up the baby, which stopped crying at once.

Edward lingered in front of Trebor Nosnibor, looking at his gorgeous jackknife and the sturdy coil of rope. Trebor was wonderful and inviting, but Edward turned away from him to walk through the mirror toward the Edward who was sitting so quietly at the big desk. There was something about this one that attracted him, something even more daring and brave than Trebor himself.

"Oh, Edward," whispered Eleanor in awe, "look at you!" His new image was the President of the United States! Truly! Edward looked at it, and felt himself turning scarlet.

"Well, look at you, too," he said.

Like his own, Eleanor's image was older, but it was very beautiful. There were graying streaks in her hair, and she was surrounded by grown sons and daughters. And her face had a combination of freckles and wrinkles so wonderful and radiant and shining that she was handsomer even than her own handsome children. Surprisingly, she looked very much like Aunt Lily.

"And look at the mirrors opening out from here!" said Eleanor. From each one of the sons and daughters a new mirror-maze opened out. And they could see that each of these children would walk naturally and easily along the right side of the maze, each one drawing out of his own private infinitude the correct thread through the labyrinth, painting and carving himself with sure hands.

But out from the new Edward there opened a range of possibilities of a more awful kind. His were not personal possibilities, but possibilities for the world. Some were very bright, and some were very dark indeed. Edward couldn't bear it any more. He looked down at the small length of himself, with his short legs and the dirt under his fingernails. "Let's not look any more," he said.

But before they turned to go, one of the images spoke to them. It was Trebor! He called to Edward, and his voice had a kind of echo in it, as though he were calling from far away, all down the corridors of the years of time they had passed through. "Edward," he said.

Edward looked up at his rejected image, feeling a little guilty. Trebor was smiling sadly at him. Then Trebor reached down and unfastened something from his belt. He reached his hand far, far out, across the intervening space, toward Eddy. Eddy reached out, too. His finger tips touched those of his image and took the object from them. He looked down at it. It was the jack-knife. "I don't need it any more," said Trebor Nosnibor, in the faraway, echoing voice.

Edward, overcome by feelings he could not express, looked up to say thank you. But the image of Trebor was retreating. All the images in the mirror-maze were rushing away from them, sweeping back into the time from which they had come.

And Eleanor and Edward were being swept back, too. Back they went, out of the mirror and out of sleep, back into the beds in the tower room of the house on Walden Street, to wake up in the present and the ordinary October morning, and sit up and look at each other.

Edward saw a redheaded girl with tangled hair, groping for her glasses, her snub childish nose generously freckled. Eleanor saw a small boy in rumpled pajamas, a boy so short that his legs still came only halfway down the bed.

Then they both looked at the big mirror across the way. It was the same as it had always been—a single sheet of glass innocently reflecting their two heads, and the window, and the diamond, and the yellow tops of the elm trees out of doors.

Edward looked down at his hands. They were folded together, clenched over something. Slowly he opened them. And there was the gift of the mirror. Trebor's knife was really there.

Edward was delighted with it. The gift might not be worth a king's ransom or a barrel of tax-money, but it was a treasure that went to his heart. He would not let himself think about that other Edward, the august Edward behind the desk in the dream—that was too great a weight to carry in his head. Instead he could play at being Trebor Nosnibor for a long time yet. Happily Eddy pulled the blades in and out, examining them. Had Ned, too, received a gift from the mirror? Could it have been as fine a one as this?

Eleanor didn't mind, either, that the dream had produced no jewels. She padded across the floor to the dresser and leaned on its marble top. Critically she examined her freckles in the mirror. Then she smiled. They weren't so bad, after all. It wasn't worth going to the trouble of stealing Aunt Lily's powder. Let her freckles glow!

14

THE STAR IN THE EAST

*I*T WAS CHRISTMAS MORNING. Uncle Freddy gave everyone embroidered mottoes he had made himself. They were a little grubby but perfectly legible. The one he had made for Aunt Lily was decorated with two big yellow footprints in satin stitch at the top, and it was a quotation from Longfellow:

LIVES OF GREAT MEN

ALL REMIND US

WE CAN MAKE OUR

LIVES SUBLIME

AND, DEPARTING,

LEAVE BEHIND US
FOOTPRINTZ IN
THE SANDS OF TIME!

"That S looks like a Z," apologized Uncle Freddy. "I got so excited along in there, I turned it around."

"Why, it's lovely, Fred, dear," said Aunt Lily.

Edward's and Eleanor's mottoes were more astronomical than anything else. They both had blue stars embroidered in lazy-daisy stitch. Edward's said,

FISH IN THE SKY!
H. D. T.

and Eleanor's said,

HITCH YOUR WAGON TO A STAR!
R. W. E.

"Those W's took ages," said Uncle Freddy proudly. Edward and Eleanor exclaimed and admired.

Eleanor had worked hard, too. She had knitted something for everybody. Aunt Lily's present was one mitten with the promise of another. Edward's was a nose-warmer that buttoned in back. Uncle Freddy's was an enormously long striped muffler. It dangled to his knees. He capered happily around in it, and kissed his niece. "It was just knit-a-row, purl-a-row," said Eleanor. "I almost forgot to stop."

Eddy had whittled his presents with the whittling blade on his new knife. (He had explained truthfully to Aunt Lily, when she asked him where it came from, that it was a hand-me-down from a friend.) Painstakingly he had carved a napkin ring for Eleanor and a letter-opener like a dagger for Aunt Lily. One of the knife blades was perfect for scraping bark, and Eddy had turned a long twig into a fishing rod like the homemade ones in the tower room. A piece of string and a fishhook completed it, and Uncle Freddy was delighted with it.

Aunt Lily's presents were store-bought. "I just went hog-wild," she said gaily. "Down with taxes—at Christmas, anyway!" Edward's was a new pair of skates, Eleanor's was a pair of cobwebby stockings, and Uncle Freddy's was a new book about the Transcendentalists. "Look," said Aunt Lily, when Uncle Freddy had fumbled the wrappings off, "there's a footnote on page seventy-four." She showed him the place. At the bottom of the page the footnote said:

[1] Hall, Frederick T., *Influences on Emerson and Thoreau.* A remarkable book by a great scholar.

Uncle Freddy took the book to the window and read the footnote to himself. "Well," he said, "well." He lifted his new muffler and dabbed at his eyes. "All that was a long time ago."

They all wore their new finery on the way to church. Even Aunt Lily's single mitten adorned one hand (the other hand was in her pocket). Eleanor's legs felt cold and beautiful in her new stockings. Uncle Freddy sported his muffler. Edward would have liked to stalk up the aisle in his new skates, but he had to be content to wear his nose-warmer.

The service in the big white church was crowded, sentimental and grand. Aunt Lily's choir outdid themselves. Timothy Shaw, the tenor, simply soared. (After the service he gave Aunt Lily a new handkerchief, bashfully—it had a pink L in one corner.) Everybody sang *The First Nowell*. Eleanor, feeling silky wrinkles around her ankles, carolled happily,

> *They lookèd up and saw a star,*
> *Shining in the East beyond them far . . .*

Benjamin Parks was standing in the next pew with his family. Eleanor pretended not to notice. But on the way out he gave her a gruff "hello." She returned it with a lovely freckled smile and squeezed Uncle Freddy's arm tight.

It had been a good day. Just before bedtime, Uncle Freddy took it into his head to go fishing with his new pole in the Mill Brook. "We'll all go," said Aunt Lily. They bundled up and walked across the frozen field. Edward put on his new skates and skated up and down.

Uncle Freddy cut a hole in the ice and let his line down into it. Then he looked up at the sky. The stars were out in crowds.

Eleanor jumped up and down to keep warm. She had changed her new stockings for her wool ones, but it was very cold. "Which star do you suppose was the star in the East?" she said.

Aunt Lily pointed at one with her new mitten. "Maybe it was Sirius," she said, "the Dog Star, following Orion across the sky. See Orion up there?" Sirius was brilliant, rising low over Emerson's house. Eleanor's astigmatism made it look like a great teardrop, welling up in the eastern sky.

"Where's the Big Dipper?" said Edward. "Oh, there it is."

They all stood with their heads thrown back. Then, suddenly, Uncle Freddy yanked his line out of the ice and started to whirl it around his head. He tossed it up at the stars. "Fish in the sky!" he cried. "Now, there's a stream to fish in! Look at those bright pebbles at the bottom!" He flung his line up again and again. "If I could catch just one star, just one, to hitch my wagon to, then how I should fly!"

His hook became entangled in his muffler. "Fred, dear," said Aunt Lily, "we'd best go in."

But Uncle Freddy struggled with his tangled line and jabbed his thumb on the fishhook. "Now, there, I've gotten blood all over it!" He flapped his muffler and sucked his thumb.

On the way to bed Edward stumbled on a ripped place in the stair carpet, and almost fell down the whole flight. "If only that silly lady lighted up," he said thickly, almost crying.

"Poor old Mrs. Truth," said Aunt Lily, helping him to his feet. They looked up at the statue on the newel post, pathetically holding up her star with its burned-out bulb.

"Poor old Eddy, you mean," said Edward.

Eleanor climbed into bed, put her head down on the pillow, thought happily for a minute about Benjamin Parks, and then fell asleep. But Edward lay awake for a little while, looking out the window. He searched for the star Aunt Lily had called the Dog Star. What was its other name—Truth? No, no, that was the other star, the one with the burned-out bulb. He had them mixed up. There it was, the Dog Star. From where he lay he could just see it at the corner of one pane of colored glass. If he moved his head a little on the pillow, the light of the star shone right through the diamond. It was like catching the sun in a pocket mirror. The diamond, ignited, blazed forth, now blue, now red, now flashing white. It became the incandescent focus of Edward's dream, and Eleanor's.

15

DIAMONDS IN THE SKY

ELEANOR WAS CALLING HIM. "Come on, lazybones, get in!" She was sitting in the dogcart.

"Just a minute," said Edward. He ran to the corner and picked up the fishing rods. They were very long for him now, but they were not heavy. He climbed in and gave one to Eleanor.

"Is there going to be a dog to pull us?" she said.

"I don't know," said Edward. He flicked his fishing rod in front of the cart. "Giddyap," he said hesitantly. They sat for a moment expectantly in the little cart, waiting for something to happen. Then something did.

The little wagon began to move. Smoothly and silently and without jolting or vibration it moved up toward the window. For a moment they were afraid they would bump it and break it, but instead they sailed right through it, just as easily as they had walked through the mirror. Had the glass dissolved? But there was the diamond in front of them. No, not the diamond, of course, but the star. It was Sirius itself, the Dog Star, and the shafts of the little wagon were hitched to it with strong rope lashings. Or was it, after all, the lamp Mrs. Truth held up, the light-bulb lamp, all plugged in and properly wired at last, and shining with a thousand candlepower? Whatever it was, it pulled them swiftly through the air and swung them in a great circle over the dark streets of Concord, over the red brick library, over the Milldam stores, over the spire of the tall white church, and over the lonesome statue of the Minuteman at the North Bridge. Then it headed back over the fantastic rooftop of their own house and over Walden Pond, and mounted toward the East.

The sky grew blue-black, and they left the shadowy earth behind. There were stars above them and below them. Their wagon floated as gently among them as though it had been a rowboat floating in the Concord River. Edward inspected his fishing pole, then flung his line over the side of the cart. It pulled to the back at once and dragged behind. He felt it give a gentle tug, and he leaned out and jerked it back in.

There was a star on the end, looking very much like a small blue-white diamond. "Look at that," he said, showing Eleanor. She fished, too, and caught a lot more. Before long they were ankle-deep in stars, which glistened and lighted up the bottom of the cart. There were so many they were in the way. The two fishermen had to push them to one side in a clutter when they wanted to move around.

"We're going down," said Eleanor. She pulled in her rod.

They were coming down in a strange place. Whether it was on the world or off it, they didn't know. It was a desert, flat and bleak and wide. Except for their own, all the stars had gone out, and the gray desert was visible by a kind of pure dawn light. Rising up out of the plain were huge black rocks like pillars. They made an irregular corridor, extending as far as the eye could see. And coming along the corridor was an endless line of men.

"Who are they?" said Eleanor. "Look, every one of them has a light."

The star that had pulled the little wagon now seemed to disengage itself. It rolled and tumbled along the desert floor. It was moving unerringly toward a great structure—a kind of immensely tall summerhouse of noble proportion, a colossal temple or bandstand supported by four columns. Up the steps of the structure bounded the star and into the hands of a woman who stood inside.

"It's Mrs. Truth," said Edward. It was, indeed. She lifted the star up over her head. Then she turned toward the long line of men.

Eleanor and Edward started to run. The sand was very hard, and delightful to run on. Eleanor, her long pigtail and her nightgown flapping out behind her, looked back over her shoulder. The sand was so hard their bare feet weren't even leaving any footprints in it. She caught Eddy's arm. "Do you suppose Ned and Nora are here?"

Then they saw them—two small figures. Ned and Nora, too, were running, running, their white legs bare. They were running toward Mrs. Truth. "This time we must catch them," said Edward, and he sprinted forward, his head thrown back, his hands clenched on his chest, his short legs pumping up and down. He soon outdistanced Eleanor. Then suddenly he had to stop. If he hadn't, he might have been stepped on. The first of the long line of men was passing by. Eleanor caught up, and together they looked out from behind one of the columns of black rock.

In their strange old skirts and draperies the men looked to them like ancient gods from some Valhalla or Mount Olympus, or gigantic prophets from the Old

Testament. The bare feet of the first man passed close by, with a heavy tread, the huge toes grasping the sand, the heels lifting, dropping granules of sand, and swinging forward to press into the sand again.

Edward nudged Eleanor. "He's leaving footprints in the sand," he said. The man approached the bandstand, or temple, or whatever it was, and climbed the steps. He gave his light to Mrs. Truth, who added it to her own. Hers burned brighter, giving off showers of sparks and shining for a moment in their two faces. Then the man passed out of the bright light and went down the other side into the dark again.

His place was taken by the next. One by one the men approached and gave their lights to Mrs. Truth. Hers would burn brighter, then fade a little—but always its brilliance was a little greater than before.

Looking up at the faces in the half-light, Eleanor and Edward found it hard to tell what races of men they were. They came alone, or in clusters, with gaps between them, or crowding on one another's heels. Behind them stretched long lines of footprints, intermingled and interwoven. Some of the marching feet left only the slightest dint-mark of toes and heels, quickly overprinted and lost in the heavier tread of those following. Some left great permanent gouges in the sand, so perfect and well-marked that others, following, walked in them.

The odd thing was that the depth of the footprint seemed to have nothing to do with the weight and height of the man. Some of the frailest left the deepest marks. Eleanor pointed this out to Edward.

"But the deeper the step, the brighter the light," said Edward, pointing to a man who was walking forward now, wearing a sort of Greek garment. He had an ugly, balding, blunt-nosed head. The light he carried flared very brightly, and his footsteps were firmly and solidly engraved in the sand. Behind him came another man, similarly dressed, and then another, stepping directly into those footprints, enlarging and widening and deepening them. One by one their three lights joined Mrs. Truth's, with blinding flashes. She smiled at them and looked up at her light. It was far more brilliant now than it had been before. But there was a brighter one coming.

"Oh, Eddy, look," said Eleanor. Far down the line they could see it coming, long before they could see the man who carried it—a radiant, gleaming sun, outshining all the others. When he finally drew near enough so that they could pick him out from the rest, his light was so glaring that they had to shade their eyes. His clothing was of a different cut from that of the three whose lights had been so bright, and it was more roughly woven. He walked heavily, his shoulders bowed a little bit as though the weight of the whole world was on them. His footsteps were so deep that his walking was very difficult. He lifted each foot with heavy labor, then sank it into the ground again. When he stood at last before Mrs. Truth and added his light to hers, her lamp burst into bright flame, lighting up the whole landscape for a moment like a sun.

There were twelve men hurrying along behind him, then troops and flocks of others, running easily in the pathway he had worn. Soon the path had broadened out over the footsteps of the earlier marchers, and the newcomers who followed had a wide and heavily travelled avenue to walk on.

And yet there were great gaps, still, in the line of men. When this happened, Mrs. Truth's beacon wasted away. She would wait patiently, her light flickering, until someone else would shuffle forward and make it shine again. But there were intervals that were very long. Edward wondered why someone hadn't organized the parade with a stop watch, and dispatched the marchers in a neat file, all of them exactly spaced so many feet apart from one another. Why didn't they all wear the same uniform and march in step? But instead they continued to come in confused bunches and clots. Often there was a throng jostling in the wake of one lone man.

The line went on and on. Gradually the clothing the men were wearing began to look different. Long tunics and monastic robes began to give way to newer fashions. There were crowds of men in bright doublets and long hose, with varieties of hats and cloaks and finery. Then, for a while, the colors became sober. The men who followed all wore black, with white ruffs or collars around their necks. Once in a while Eleanor could identify a grave history-book face.

All at once she whispered in Eddy's ear, "An American!" There he was, a forefather—dressed in stern black, walking solemnly and heavily, carrying a weighty book. Behind him were other ancestral faces, and soon the citizens of the New World began to be numerous among the others. They began to make their own lane in the broad highway. Their somber black was given up for lighter colors in jackets and knee breeches and vests, but then it came back again in long trousers and tall hats and frock coats.

Edward saw them first, two faces that looked like friends. "It's Waldo!" he said. "And there's Henry, right behind him!"

"How bright their lights are!" said Eleanor. "Oh, if only Uncle Freddy could see them."

Here were his idols, large as life, not in marble but in flesh and blood—Emerson, the sage of Concord, with his gentle smile and narrow scholar's shoulders— Thoreau, his well-worn clothes hanging easily about his small frame, his face calm and a little pugnacious, with its large eyes and commanding nose. Eleanor and Edward watched them hungrily, for Uncle Freddy's sake, until they were out of sight.

Then there was a surprise. Someone much farther down the line, half-hidden by a horde of other marchers, caught Eleanor's attention. There was something delightfully familiar about him, something warmly, charmingly recognizable! Eleanor wanted to run to meet him. Who could it be?

It was Uncle Freddy. He was here, after all, marching in the same line with his heroes! But he was a very different Uncle Freddy. Eleanor fell back behind Edward and watched him approach in awed silence. The Uncle Freddy *they* knew had a face that seemed to have come apart into a sort of miscellaneous collection of features. *This* Uncle Freddy's face was all put together again. The features were knit by a look of calm sanity, the eyes were clear with a keen steadiness. He walked with dignity up the steps of Mrs. Truth's airy house and added his light to hers. It gave her light more splendor for a moment. They hated to see him go.

But after him came many more. There were many lanes of marchers now. Some had come by other routes, paths laid down by pioneers in other sorts of clothes, odd clothes of bizarre and foreign make, Asian garments,

Oriental silks and robes, or the rags and tatters of mystics and ascetics. Some of these paths had run together with one another, but some had deepened and widened in isolation, without blending so much as a grain of sand. Was that another pioneer, carving out a path for himself outside all the rest? Eleanor turned to look.

No—he wasn't marching down the corridor at all. He was approaching from another direction, across the flat desert floor. It was the direction from which they had come themselves. "Look," said Eleanor, nudging Edward.

"Where?" said Edward. Then he saw it, the distant silhouette of a running man. He carried a light, and he was holding it over his head, and turning his head this way and that as though he were looking for something.

It was the shape of his head that told them who he was. "It's Prince Krishna," said Edward, "and he's looking for Ned and Nora!"

Prince Krishna came closer. He was running lightly, but his shoes were leaving deep footprints in the sand. Round about him he flung his light. His fine face was lined with anxiety. Turning this way and that, he was about to pass on beyond Mrs. Truth's house, when for the first time, she turned away from the advancing line of men and looked at him. She reached out a hand to him. Prince Krishna paused and looked at her doubtfully. Then, slowly, he approached. She smiled at him encouragingly.

But just then a wind rose up and spun across the sand. It was a strange, coarse, ugly wind. Prince Krishna quickly put up one hand to shield his light, but he was too late. The wind nipped it out, then went screaming on in gusts across the way he had come, seeking out his footprints, and obliterating and destroying them, one by one, until the sand was as smooth as though he had never been.

"No!" cried Eleanor. "No, no!"

She woke up to find herself looking wildly across the room into Edward's face. He, too, was wide awake and sitting bolt upright. His eyes were staring into hers. He, too, was shouting, "No!"

For a moment they stared at each other. Then Edward jumped out of bed and ran to the big Jack-in-the-box in the corner. He gave it a kick. "It was his fault," he cried. The box flew open, and the ugly Jack sprang out. Its heavy nose hit Eddy. He grabbed it on its recoil, and shook it by the neck. "Let them go!" he shouted. "Let Ned and Nora and Prince Krishna go!"

"Oh, Eddy, don't!" said Eleanor. She slid out of bed, too, and put her arms around her brother's waist, trying to pull him loose. They fell over together, with the Jack smashing down on top. Then, tussling and straining, they rammed it back inside the box again and closed the cover down and hooked it firmly. Eddy sat on it and banged it with his fists.

Eleanor watched him and worried. Had there been a kind of vengeful look on the face of the Jack-in-the-box, or had she imagined it? But she was being silly. After all, it was only a toy. And it was put away safely, with its lid hooked shut.

On the way down to breakfast Eleanor stopped on the stairs beside Mrs. Truth and looked at her again. Mrs. Truth was gazing straight ahead, just as usual, through the glass pane of the front door. It was just as if she expected to see one of the marchers from the dream come walking up the front steps, wipe his feet on the doormat, knock on the door, and come in, to light her lamp for her. But her star remained bleak and dark, and her welcoming arm carried no promise but that of two umbrellas and Uncle Freddy's new muffler.

Eleanor sighed. The day after Christmas was always a little sad. After breakfast she went back upstairs with Eddy, and half-heartedly they looked for the "diamonds in the sky." They had fished them up themselves, in the dream, and left them heaped in the bottom of the dog cart. But of course there were no stars there. They looked at the little cart, lying motionless with its shafts resting on the floor. Idly Edward poked around in the cart for a false bottom. There wasn't any.

"Ned and Nora probably found them first," said Eleanor.

"But where do you suppose they put them?" said Edward.

Eleanor had an inspiration. "I'll bet they put them in the treasure chest! 'Eye of bird, eye of fowl, hides the treasure chest.' And that's why Aunt Lily never found any jewels in their pockets!"

It sounded plausible. But where was the treasure chest? As the days wore on and as the weeks passed by, both Eleanor and Edward began privately to feel that the whole thing was probably very silly, and to wonder if, really and truly, they hadn't better give up.

16

WHO SENT THE VALENTINE?

FOR NEARLY TWO LONG months there were no more clues, no more dreams, and, of course, no treasures. Aunt Lily in the meantime taught twice as many pupils as before and put in the bank as much of her earnings as she could. They had to eat, the four of them, and Aunt Lily fed them all well and thriftily, but there was very little money for anything else.

Certainly not for new clothes. The old ones had to do. Edward didn't mind at all, but Eleanor did. Most of all she hated her winter stockings. Not the new ones, of course, but the heavy ones that had to be worn for warmth. Eleanor always rolled them down like dough- nuts around her ankles when she got to school and then rolled them up again before coming home. Even during the Valentine's Day snowstorm she rolled them down, and she didn't remember to pull them up after school until she came into her own front hall. "Don't tell on me, Mrs. Truth," whispered Eleanor, tugging away at them. One of the elastic bands that held them up snapped, and the stocking sagged stupidly. Eleanor hung her coat and hat over Mrs. Truth's arm to dry. Then she walked drearily into the kitchen, one sock up and one sock down.

"I only got three," said Eleanor, dropping three damp envelopes on the table.

"Three what?" said Aunt Lily.

"Three Valentines," said Eleanor. "All penny ones, too." She pulled them out. "From Miss Archer, Lucy Smith, and Tommy Whipple. And they all sent Valentines to everybody in the class. Mary Jane Broom got fourteen!"

Aunt Lily looked at the Valentines. One of them was a dog with a movable tail. "My tail wags for you, Valentine!" it said.

"Why, I think they're very nice, Eleanor dear," said Aunt Lily.

Eleanor sat slumped in a kitchen chair, sipping a cup of cocoa and feeling sorry for herself. "If I had pretty dresses like Mary Jane Broom, I bet I would have got more," she found herself saying.

Uncle Freddy dunked a piece of toast in his cocoa and sucked it noisily. "Henry," he said, "despises fine clothes!" He gave his niece a pat. "Old shoes will serve a hero!" he said.

"But I'm not a hero," thought Eleanor crossly to herself. She looked down at her strong ugly boots. Who wanted to be a hero in old shoes? She wanted to be like Mary Jane Broom, with pretty dresses and shoes with bows and lots of Valentines, or like Cinderella, for that matter, with a beautiful gown and glass slippers and a ball to go to.

Eddy came home from school. He was completely insensitive to Valentines or the lack of them. He hurled himself into the house and out again, to wallow happily in the drifts with his sled and his friend Abraham Hotchkiss.

It was during this noisy interval that the Valentine appeared, standing cocked up in its envelope on Mrs. Truth's open book. Eleanor found it. Had someone slipped in the door and put it there? Surely not Eddy? On the front of it was her own name, "Miss Eleanor Hall." Who could have sent it? It wasn't like the penny ones from school. She could tell that from the envelope, which was a big creamy square. Eleanor opened it eagerly.

Inside was the most beautiful Valentine she had ever

seen. It was a confection of paper lace and freestanding parts that pulled out in front of one another, and cupid boys with bows and arrows and red ribbon. In the middle were two red satin hearts shot through with a gilt arrow, and written across them were the words, "To one I love."

"Oh," breathed Eleanor. Her heavy shoes suddenly seemed as giddy as glass slippers. On the back of the Valentine were the words, "From one who admires you deeply." Who could have sent it? Surely not Benjamin Parks? Everybody knew he liked Mary Jane Broom, you could tell by the way he was always teasing her. But then who else? A mysterious admirer! Eleanor pressed the Valentine against the front of her middy.

There was Uncle Freddy on the stairs beside Percival. He was watching her. Eleanor ran up and showed him the Valentine.

"Yes, yes," said Uncle Freddy. But he hardly looked at it. Instead he looked brightly at Eleanor and patted her cheek.

All of a sudden Eleanor knew. Uncle Freddy had sent it! Not Benjamin Parks! Not some unknown, mysterious admirer! Eleanor's heart fell. Her eyes filled. She kissed Uncle Freddy quickly and ran downstairs to the kitchen to Aunt Lily. She buried her face in Aunt Lily's apron and pushed her thin knuckles into Aunt Lily's arms. Aunt Lily looked at the Valentine and sighed. Then she sat down with Eleanor in her lap and rocked her back and forth.

"It was my Valentine, once," said Aunt Lily. "*He* sent it to me."

Eleanor sobbed. She nodded, bumping her head up and down under Aunt Lily's chin. "He" was Prince Krishna, of course.

Aunt Lily pulled something off the front of the envelope. Eleanor's name had been written on a separate pasted piece of paper. Underneath were the words, "For Lily." Of course, thought Eleanor, she should have known—the writing inside was Prince Krishna's.

"At first we were all very good friends, Krishna and Fred and I," said Aunt Lily, looking at the Valentine. "Then after a while he stopped talking to me at all, and just blushed and stammered and wouldn't even look at me, except when he thought I didn't know. But I knew. I could feel his eyes on the back of my head. Then on Valentine's Day he gave me this—and the next day he asked me to marry him."

"Did you say yes?" wept Eleanor. She was crying for Aunt Lily now, not for herself.

Aunt Lily looked out the window at the snowstorm.

"Yes, I did," she said. She pulled her handkerchief out of her pocket and wiped Eleanor's wet cheeks. "We were walking in the snow."

There was a sharp knock at the front door, and Eleanor slid down from Aunt Lily's lap. It was Leonard Updyke, come for his lesson. Aunt Lily blew her nose and went forth to meet him, and Eleanor started slowly upstairs. She had no wish to hear him murder "The Happy Farmer." She climbed all the way up to the tower room, took off her shoes, and flung herself down on her bed.

Then she pulled open all the freestanding parts of Aunt Lily's Valentine and set it carefully on the table beside the bed, next to the big block castle. Out-of-doors she could see Eddy and Abraham Hotchkiss. They were jostling white clods of snow off trees. The clods turned to clouds of white powder and mingled with the falling snow, which was coming down less heavily now—it was just big clusters of flakes falling together lazily.

The white winter light from the out-of-doors fell upon the window. By some trick of light the diamond in the middle picked up a reflection from one of the panes of red glass, and passed it along into the room, so that the walls and ceiling glowed a soft red.

"Red is for Valentine hearts and love," thought

Eleanor. She could feel herself drifting off into sleep, snow-drifting over pillows and billows of white. And she could feel that a dream was on its way, a dream she was to have all to herself—a Valentine dream, all white and red, with ribbons and bows, and lover's knots, and hearts entwined.

17

THE BRIDE OF SNOW

THE SNOW WAS FALLING in the dream, too. And of course since she was small enough to go right into the Valentine, she could see the separate flakes in all their crystalline perfection. The Valentine towered over her. Behind it was another high lacy square, and behind that, another, and then another and another. Before her they stood in line like giant frames, each one with its cutout heart to walk through, like Moon-gates in a Japanese garden.

But the Valentine wasn't standing on the window sill. It was towering whitely and fragilely up to the bare gray elm tree tops on Monument Square. And through the empty hearts she could see a tableau as pretty as a picture. In the middle was a huge snowman with a red muffler around his neck. In front of the snowman, pelting it with snowballs, were Ned and Nora. Nora wore a little red cape and hood and Ned was bundled into a heavy sweater, with red mittens and a red hat with a long tail. And behind them, behind the snowman, rising up in the center of the tableau, was the Civil War Memorial obelisk. Snow had fallen on the letters of the inscription, accenting and outlining them in white. Eleanor knew the words by heart—they said, "FAITHFUL UNTO DEATH."

She began climbing through the heart-shaped openings. It was slow going. She had to lift her legs high as she climbed over, sinking deep into the downy snow on the other side. Her stocking was still sagging, and she hung onto the top of it through her skirt, feeling awkward. She called to Ned and Nora, but her voice was muffled in the snow, and they didn't hear.

Only two more Valentines to climb through! Eleanor flopped along, full of hope. Perhaps this time she would really catch up with the lost children, and play with them, and bring them back home with her again!

But that was not to be. Not this time. Nora threw a snowball at the snowman and missed. Then Ned threw one, very hard, and hit the snowman's round head so squarely that it nearly toppled off. The head was shoved back on the snowman's hard-packed body, and it reared up there at a new angle, looking oddly threatening and weird. Then Eleanor, with one leg up over the next Valentine opening, stopped. Had she really seen what she thought she saw? In a horrible slushing way the snowman seemed to be moving forward, clawing with its twig arms at Ned. Nora and Ned started to run away from it, packing snowballs and throwing them as they went. Nora's all went wild, but Ned's were aimed well and truly. They hit the snowman again and again. At last he seemed to stop, frozen and still again. Ned and Nora were gone, but someone else was coming.

Eleanor stood behind the last Valentine and watched. There were two people coming, a man and a girl, and she could see that they would meet directly in front of her, right in front of the snowman and the monument, to make a charming sentimental picture within the pretty heart-shaped frame.

The first was Prince Krishna. He was walking along, looking overwhelmingly handsome, wearing a bright red turban and a grave black coat. There was a little book in his hand, and he was studying it so carefully that he didn't see where he was going, and he collided with the girl. Eleanor couldn't see at first who the girl was. She was tall, and she wore a gray scarf pulled around her head and a smart close-fitting jacket. Then the girl pulled off her scarf, and her red hair tumbled down from the place where it was caught up in a big bow. It was Aunt Lily, the pretty young Aunt Lily in the album!

Prince Krishna's face was flaming. He dropped his book, and they both bent to pick it up, bumping their heads together. Aunt Lily stood up, laughing. But Prince Krishna's face when he stood up had an expression so serious and loving that she stopped laughing and bent her head. He took her hand, with a beautiful gentle gesture, and spoke to her softly. Aunt Lily looked down at the snow, then gave him her other hand. Then she looked up at him and smiled, and turned quickly and hurried away. Her long skirts passed near Eleanor, and, looking up at her, Eleanor could see that her face glowed with happiness. Prince Krishna just stood where he was, his face, too, radiant with love, as he watched her go.

Eleanor sucked in her breath. Behind Prince Krishna the snowman towered high, and now it was mushing forward again, its stick-arms vibrating. Why did it look so different from that same jolly snowman that turns up, always, under the mittened hands of any child playing in the snow? The features were made of small sticks, and some trick of twiggy growth gave the snowman's nose a downward hook, and the mouth a wicked grin—

"Watch out! Oh, watch out!" Had Prince Krishna heard her? He had started up and set off again at a brisk walk. The snowman was left behind. Then all at once it ran together and melted into a sodden heap.

Eleanor climbed over the last of the Valentine gates and hurried after Prince Krishna, tugging at her stocking. Where was he going? What was he doing? He was reaching up and doing something with his hands.

He was gathering snowflakes! They were still falling, in enormous flat cartwheel crystals. Prince Krishna collected them in armfuls as he walked. He was heading for an open field. Eleanor struggled after him, and found her way among the stubbled grass. The snowflakes wafted gently against its icy bristles and clung to them, resting upon clusters of other great crystals, angularly cocked or hooked together or layered upon one another.

What was Prince Krishna doing now, with his armfuls of snowflakes? He was weaving them together. He strung a ruffled length of them, like angelic laundry, from the prongs of a barbed-wire fence. He tossed some onto fence post tops, where they sat on little pillows of snow like frozen antimacassars, and then he began weaving it into a wide fabric and draping it loosely over his arm. Was it the warmth of his fingers that melted together the tips of the crystal arms? Or did he somehow mesh and hook them into one another?

Prince Krishna stood now at the edge of the field in a little clearing surrounded by a bushy growth of young saplings. Deftly, surely, swiftly he was setting about a new piece of work. Upward from the surface of the snow he was building something, drawing up between his hands the tissues of snow that he had woven. Eleanor could only breathe, "Oh," and "Ah."

It was a dress, purely white, fragilely strong, gather and fold and pleat constructed of a lace more delicate than any Eleanor had ever seen. The skirt was a softly falling cylinder with a flowing train, narrowing around the waist, and then flaring out to encase a bodice, and narrowing again to form a little lacy band around the throat. The sleeves were thin tunnels of woven snow, and above, suspended from pine boughs, a tissue of veiling drooped forward over the airy volume where the head should be and blew behind in a billow of lacy mist.

It was Aunt Lily's wedding dress. It was far and away the most beautiful wedding dress ever worn by any bride in the world. Prince Krishna stood back to look at it. Then he strode to the barbed-wire fence and caught up some of the lacy ruffles he had hung there. Eleanor saw his blood come, and drop on the snow. He had pricked his finger on the sharp hooked wire, but he didn't know it. He lifted the ruffling and laid it around the neck of the wedding dress. A drop of blood fell from his finger and stained the bodice of the wedding dress. It colored a snowflake on the left side of the front. Prince Krishna turned pale when he saw it and tried to pull out the red-stained crystals. But they were hooked fast together. Instead he pulled something out of his pocket, something red and shining, and pinned it over the place to cover it. It was a ruby brooch. Then, carefully, and with a look of sorrow on his face, Prince Krishna detached his gleaming gown from the trees, and carried the dress away, cradled lovingly in his arms.

The dream was over. Eleanor woke up and stared up at the ceiling of the tower room. The soft red light from the window had deepened to crimson. "Red is for Prince Krishna's blood," thought Eleanor.

How long had she been asleep? She rolled over and looked out of the window. Eddy and Abraham Hotchkiss were still rolling in the snow. Downstairs Leonard Updyke was grinding out the scale of D Major, and always forgetting to sharp the C. Hardly any time at all. Eleanor sat up and rubbed her eyes. There were patterns under her eyelids when she did that, patterns like snowflakes.

Was there a real snowflake wedding dress? If there was, then it was "the bride of snow"! And the brooch was the flawless ruby! Eleanor knew one place to look for the treasure, and she went straight to it. Leonard Updyke was just banging into "The Happy Farmer" when she found the old dressmaker's dummy, standing dustily in its place in the corner of the attic.

Da-*da*, da-*dah*, da-da-da-*da*-da-da, Leonard pounded, his left hand making sloppy oom-pah chords. Eleanor hummed the tune and undid some of the pins that held the dummy closely wrapped in ugly black muslin. One corner was free now, and she peeked in. There was a gleam of white. It was lace, the softest cloudiest lace! "Da-*da*-da-da, da-*da*-da-da, da-*da*-*da*-*da*!" shouted Eleanor. She had found it! She ran down the attic stairs and the back stairs and out the kitchen door and into the snow in her stocking feet, shouting for Eddy.

Abraham Hotchkiss agreeably went home, and soon Eleanor and Edward were back beside the dummy in the attic, pulling out pins. Standing there in her sopping stockings, Eleanor told Eddy as much of her dream as she could remember. At last they had freed the black shroud of its pins, and together, very carefully, they could lift it off.

It was Aunt Lily's snowflake wedding dress. The train was still pinned up, and the veil was folded over the top. Reverently Eleanor unpinned them, and shook them loose. To her surprise the delicate lace was not cold but warm. She took the veil to the window and held it up to the light. Surely it was just very beautiful crochet, or some extraordinary lace made by nimble-fingered old women in Ireland or France or Belgium? But it was not. "Look," said Edward, "every little piece of the pattern is different."

It was true. They looked and looked, holding up corner after corner of the veil, the sleeves, the train. Nowhere could they find two elements alike. Always, always they were distinct, unique, endlessly different exquisite hexagons.

The front of the figure was still in shadow. Was the ruby there? There was a dark splotch on the front. Eleanor reached for it and touched it. The ruby was gone, of course. (It would be! Anything they could turn into spot cash was always missing.) Ever so carefully Eleanor turned the dummy toward the light. Prince Krishna's blood was a small brown stain. The blood was dry, but a sense of tragedy welled out of it. "Look," said Eleanor, "it's right over Aunt Lily's heart."

On his way to bed that night Edward saw something white sticking out from under the front door. He pulled it out and looked at it. "Hey, Eleanor," he said, "here's another Valentine for you!"

Eleanor took it and looked at it suspiciously. Had Uncle Freddy sent it? But he hadn't. Nor had Eddy, or Aunt Lily.

It was one of the cheap penny ones from the ten-cent store. Inside the envelope was a Valentine that showed a funny apple-cheeked boy with an enormous dish full of red cherries. The printed message said, "Life would be just a bowl of cherries, if you would be my Valentine." On the back, in very tiny, faint pencil, were the initials, "B.P."

18

THE CHAMBERED NAUTILUS

S NOW IN FEBRUARY IS THE proper thing to have. Snow in March is too much of a good thing. Dirty glaciers of it surrounded the house, and icy gray peninsulas extended across the front yard, decomposing in sandy slush along the sidewalk on warm days, and glassing up again on cold ones. Winter hung on like a bitter grudge. Would it never end?

"You know where I'd like to be right now?" said Edward. He was playing with his jackknife on the front porch. The narrow blade was perfect for throwing. It nearly always stuck point-down. His throwing hand was bare, and it was whitish-blue with cold.

"No, where?" said Eleanor.

"Lying on the beach, with my bare feet digging in the sand and warm sunshine shining on my stomach and—"

"Oh, stop!" said Eleanor.

But Edward went on, while he narrowed his eyes and threw the knife over and over again at a certain mark in the board-floor. He would get up after a while, he said, and run along the edge of the water, which would be warm; and then he would wade in and find shells; and he would look for dead smelly fish-carcasses higher up on the beach; then he would plunge into the water and swim rapidly out to sea, and dive underwater and battle with a shark, wrestling with it violently and finally sending it to Davy Jones with his trusty jackknife. (Trebor Nosnibor had obviously taken over here— Edward Hall couldn't even swim.)

Eleanor leaned back on the peeling paint of a knobby porch pillar and closed her eyes. "I'd just like to hear the sound of the waves coming in," she said.

Edward stopped with his knife in throwing position and looked at her. "You can do that already," he said. He folded up his knife and went indoors and ran upstairs. In a moment he came down again with the big seashell from the tower room in his hand. Eleanor stood in the parlor, with her heavy coat unbuttoned, and held the big shell cupped to her ear. "Do you hear it?" said Edward.

At first she couldn't hear it, then she could—a dim roar like the noise of the surf, as though the shell had stored up and bottled the sound of the ocean from which it came, and now was letting it out again, softly. "Let me try," said Eddy.

Eleanor watched him. "Look," she said, squinting at the shell, "there's something written on it." Eddy took it away from his ear and turned it over in his hands.

"So there is," he said. He read it aloud—"*'Build thee more stately mansions, O my soul!'*"

Uncle Freddy popped his head through the parlor curtain. "That's perfect!" he said. "Another motto! Just let me jot that down!" He disappeared and then burst through again, carrying his embroidery hoop. "Why didn't I think of that myself?" he said. He took notes rapidly in purple thread, leaning over to look at the inscription on the shell.

"What does it mean, Uncle Freddy?" said Eleanor.

"Well, of course, Waldo thought of it first," said Uncle Freddy. He bowed and waved his hoop graciously at Emerson's white marble bust. "But Oliver Wendell Holmes wrote *The Chambered Nautilus*."

Uncle Freddy went on to explain it in his own

161

singular way, trying to draw pictures rapidly with his needle and thread on the embroidery hoop. Finding that too slow he made a set of hasty pencil scratches on his cuff. Eleanor and Edward gradually began to understand that the shell itself was called a Chambered Nautilus and that the little creature that had lived in it had built it all himself. As he grew larger he had sealed off a room behind him and built himself a bigger one, and he went on and on building larger chambers for himself until he had finished building the big shell they held in their hands. It was just chamber spiralling out beyond chamber.

Uncle Freddy tapped his pencil on the picture he had drawn on his cuff. "The ship of pearl," he said. Then he tossed pencil, thimble, needle, thread and hoop to the four corners of the room, bounded up on the sofa and declaimed the poem by heart.

> *This is the ship of pearl, which, poets feign,*
> *Sails the unshadowed main,—*
> *The venturous bark that flings*
> *On the sweet summer wind its purpled wings*
> *In gulfs enchanted, where the Siren sings,*
> *And coral reefs lie bare,*
> *Where the cold sea-maids rise to sun*
> *their streaming hair. . . .*

162

Year after year beheld the silent toil
    That spread his lustrous coil;
    Still, as the spiral grew,
He left the past year's dwelling for the new,
Stole with soft step its shining archway through,
    Built up its idle door,
Stretched in his last-found home,
        and knew the old no more. . . .

Build thee more stately mansions, O my soul,
    As the swift seasons roll!
    Leave thy low-vaulted past!
Let each new temple, nobler than the last,
Shut thee from heaven with a dome more vast,
    Till thou at length art free,
Leaving thine outgrown shell
        by life's unresting sea!

"Say," said Edward, "that's pretty good!"

Uncle Freddy got down off the sofa and scrabbled around on his hands and knees for his embroidery hoop. "It was Waldo, of course, who gave him the idea," he said.

That night the moonlight shining into the tower room was softened by gauzy veils of cloud. Tossed and shadowed a little by the cold trees outside, it sent over the small room a shimmering mottled light, like sunlight in water, or mother-of-pearl. And so the adventure came just for the asking. It was the most dangerous affair so far, but in the beginning it was very much like Eddy's pretty daydream, with the bright blue sky and the friendly sandy shore—

19

THE TREASURE ROUNDED BY THE SEA

THEY WERE WALKING EASILY along the edge of the ocean.

"The tide is out," said Edward. He could tell, because much of the upward sweep of the beach had been left wet and hard by the ebbing water. "Why are we going this way?" he said. He turned around and walked backwards. "Why not that way?"

Eleanor glanced hastily over her shoulder, and walked quickly on. "No," she said, "this is the way we should go." Ahead of them a long line of rocks thrust out into the water. "Let's see what's on the other side," she said.

Eddy ran splashing in and out of the shallow water.

Since it was low tide, there was not much surf. The water came in and went out quietly, almost without white crests on the waves. It curled and foamed in small bubbles around his ankles. His feet sank pleasantly into the gray sand as the water withdrew. He found a dead whale.

"Look, look!" he shouted, dancing around it. It was enormous. The sea lifted the dead body a little and carried it a little farther from the shore.

"That's not a whale," said Eleanor, walking past it and making a face. "It's a mackerel."

Eddy poked it with his foot. Of course it was. They were small again, and the fish was normal size. He hated to leave it. "Come on," said Eleanor.

But then she stopped and stared at the sand. There was a line of footprints, running ahead of them, hugging the lapping tide line. Footprints in the sand! Again! But these were children's footprints, no bigger than their own. "See!" she said, pointing.

Eddy ran along the line of footprints, bent over, looking at them. "It's two sets," he said. "I'll bet it's theirs, Ned's and Nora's!" He stood up and glanced at the receding water. "And they must have been made since the last tide!"

The waves, too, had left their mark. Eddy could see the game that had been played. The double line of small footprints dodged in and out, running along the edge of a wave to its high-water line, then chasing it back. That was a game he and Eleanor loved to play, too. What fun the four of them could have, playing it, all together!

Eleanor climbed up on a big boulder and shaded her eyes with her hand, looking along the beach. The shoreline stretched in a shallow curve, making a long crescent that cusped out in a line of rocks, far away. "I see them," she said. "At least I think I do."

Eddy climbed up beside her and gripped the boulder with his toes. "Yes," he said, "that's them, all right." His sharper eyes could see two specks that were children. They were frolicking in and out of the water, far away, and calling to each other with light shouts that were nothing more than threadlike sounds above the soft noises of the surf.

As they watched, the little figures began to run. Edward and Eleanor scrambled down from the boulder and started after them. Blurred by the distance, the scraps of color that were Ned and Nora faded and reappeared to Eleanor's vision the way a lost gas balloon does as it rises higher and higher in the sky—now you can see it, and you can still see it, and you can still see it, then you can no longer see it, and you search the sky for it—then you catch sight of it again, and watch it steadfastly—and you see it, and you see it, and you see it—and then all at once you can no longer see it at all.

They were gone. Again! Even Eddy lost sight of them, and he slowed down at last and stopped. "Oh, well," he said, disheartened.

Gone, gone, whispered the water, purling up and sucking back around their legs.

They turned away from the water, then, and started splashing their way up the sloping beach. And then for the first time they saw what stood there, safely above the highest mark of the tide.

It was the shell, the Chambered Nautilus. Its curving mottled sides reared high above the sand. The small footprints of Ned and Nora were all around it. Eleanor and Edward approached it, and stood and looked at it.

The great lip of the shell extended toward them. Eleanor climbed up on it and stood up. Eddy climbed up, too. The huge scooping surface tilted down and back, and around a curving wall. They wanted to see what lay behind it. Eddy looked. "There's an opening here," he said.

"Let's go in," said Eleanor. She let Eddy crawl through first, and then she slipped in behind him. They found themselves in a high room, oddly shaped, like a shallow S. The shell walls were thin and translucent, and the room was filled with light.

"Let's just see what's in the next room," said

Eleanor. "See, there's another door."

They crawled through the door and found themselves in a room exactly like the one they had left, only
a little smaller in size. That room, too, had another door,
and through that door they could see still another, curving off a little to the right. They went through them both,
and then through many more, entering each time a
smaller room, and winding closer and closer to the heart
of the shell. At last the chambers were so small that they
had to stoop, then bend right over, then crawl on hands
and knees.

The last chamber was filled with pearls! Pearls as
big as baseballs, pearls as big as grapefruit, pearls as big
as melons! Their satin surfaces were faintly pink, or
blue, or gray, or yellow. "It's the treasure from the sea,"
breathed Eleanor.

"Look at this one," said Edward. He held up a white
one that fitted his hand like a baseball and pretended to
throw it.

"That's just a seed pearl," said Eleanor. "How do you
like this?" She held her arms around a huge pink pearl.
Her fingers wouldn't meet on the other side. It was like
holding a pink cloud.

Then she gave a little scream. The whole shell was
tilting. She dropped the pearl and fell backwards, with a
tumble of pearls and her brother piling on top of her.

The room darkened.

They couldn't see, but they knew perfectly well what had happened. A huge hand had picked up the shell, roughly, and was carrying it—where? Suddenly the motion stopped. There was a grating noise, and the shell came to rest, subsiding in the sand at a little angle. The shadowy hand withdrew, and their small treasure-laden chamber was filled with light again.

Whose hand had it been? Where were they? "Let's go now," said Eleanor. She rolled over and started filling her arms with pearls. Then she put them all down and picked up the big pink one. Eddy started gathering an assortment of different sizes and colors.

"Where's the door?" said Eleanor. Kneeling with her pink pearl in her lap, she stared at the wall through which they had come. There was no opening there.

"Maybe it was in the other wall," said Eddy. They groped around in the tiny space, bumping into each other, trying one wall after another, then the ceiling, and finally kicking the pearls this way and that to hammer the floor. There was no door, anywhere.

For a moment they just sat and stared at each other. In the silence they could hear a new sound. It was the ocean. Its murmuring had been soft and indistinct, like the sound of someone memorizing poetry quietly under his breath. Now all at once it was a dull roar.

"We must have been put down nearer the water," said Eleanor.

"And the tide is coming in!" said Edward.

They were trapped. They searched the walls again. Then they battered them again. But it was no use. At last they sat back and just waited. Eleanor leaned against the wall and stared at her bare feet. She thought about what it would be like to be carried out to sea. If they were tossed around by the waves she would be seasick. Everything made her seasick, even the swings at school.

Eddy crouched beside her, listening to the sound of the water. The noise had diminished again. The roaring must have been the first big wave. It might be a while before there was another. He kicked a pearl. Waiting like this would be boring. If they were never to get out, what would they do with themselves? To pass the time he whispered the alphabet to himself, backwards— "ZYXWVUTSRQPONMLKJIHGFEDCBA." With the "A," he felt the wall fall away behind him, and he tumbled through, falling on his back in the next room.

"The door!" cried Eleanor. She squirmed through, too, and slid on her knees across the tipped floor to the opposite side. What had happened to the next door? It, too, was gone. Again there was nothing but the delicate membrane of mother-of-pearl. What had made the first door come back again?

"All I did was say the alphabet backwards," said Edward. "Maybe it's talking backwards that does it." He rattled off a backwards sentence, "Nepo pu! Ereh I ma gniklat sdrawkcab, nepo pu!"

"Nepo pu," echoed Eleanor. But nothing happened. She screamed it, "NEPO PU, NEPO PU!"

Outside the sound of the ocean was growing louder again. No door appeared. "No," said Eddy, "that's not it."

Eleanor stared at the blank wall. Then she tried something else. "Little Boy Blue, come blow your horn, the sheep's in the meadow, the cow's in the corn—" She stopped, and together they watched a little opening appear in the wall, just big enough for them to crawl through. "You have to *think* something," said Eleanor triumphantly, "something special!"

They had found the trick. "I've got a good one," said Eddy, staring at the third blank wall. "It's a joke. What squeals louder than a pig stuck in a barn door?"

"Two pigs," said Eleanor scornfully. "That will never work." But it did. The wall opened up. There was a door.

"It likes jokes!" said Eddy.

"And poetry!" said Eleanor. She shouted some— "I-fear-thee-ancient-mariner-I-fear-thy-skinny-hand-and-thou-art-long-and-lank-and-brown-as-is-the-ribbed-sea-sand!" Another door opened.

For a while they had good luck with everything they

tried. "What's black and white and read all over? A newspaper!" That worked. So did the first four lines of *The Village Blacksmith.* So did *The Purple Cow.* Then suddenly nothing worked.

The Three Little Kittens didn't work. Neither did *Humpty Dumpty.* Desperately Eddy tried to remember another joke. He couldn't think of any, so he made one up. "What meows louder than a cat on the back fence? Two cats!" That didn't work either. "What's happened?" said Eddy.

Eleanor looked up at the ceiling of the chamber in which they were kneeling. "I think this one is big enough to stand up in," she said. They tried it, and Eleanor's head just grazed the top. It was a relief to stand upright. And all at once, Eleanor knew what was happening. It was like Uncle Freddy's poem about the Chambered Nautilus. "Build thee more stately mansions, O my soul!" Each chamber asked of them something bigger and better, just as the sea-animal that had built this shell had been forced to build himself bigger and bigger rooms because he was growing all the time. Their thoughts, too, were supposed to grow. *Little Boy Blue* and Eddy's jokes had been good enough for the smallest chambers. But now they must think of things that were nobler and nobler!

She explained this theory to Eddy, and they stood in

the new room, trying to think noble thoughts. Foolishly, all that Eleanor could think of for five long minutes (as the incoming tide rose higher and higher, and the highest waves came nearer and nearer) was, "It's raining, it's pouring, the old man is snoring." Edward tried multiplying 3745 by 463 in his head. No door opened.

"But we're only halfway out," said Eddy. "We need at least ten more good ones."

"Ten, ten!" said Eleanor. "The Ten Commandments, I learned them last year in Sunday School!"

Six of the ten commandments got them through six doors. That was all Eleanor could remember. She tried "Honor thy father and mother" over again on the seventh, but it didn't work.

"What about some of those things Uncle Freddy is always saying?" said Edward.

Eleanor remembered a funny one: "Call not Nature dumb!" It worked fine. And so did "Old shoes will serve a hero." Eddy tried singing Aunt Lily's hymn, "Oh, for a faith that will not shrink," and that worked, too! In a moment they found themselves standing in the loftiest chamber of all.

"This must be the last," said Edward. The great room was filled with milky light. But now they could summon no thoughts at all, large or small, except the urgent one that they wanted desperately to get out. Edward couldn't think of anything. Eleanor put her hands to her head and shook it, but nothing came out except *The Night Before Christmas*. And that wasn't good enough.

And no wonder! Eleanor looked around. What thought could possibly be too large for this room? The spacious gently curving walls led up to an arched vault, a gracious dome, its pearly translucence softly filtering the light. It was a pure and lovely chamber, a "mansion" more stately than the last and than all the rest.

She despaired. And suddenly their situation became more dangerous. The beautiful chamber was lifted up by the water, there was for a moment an airy buoyant sensation, a slight wallowing, and then they subsided again, tipped over to one side.

"We'll be washed out to sea!" said Eleanor.

"Yes," said Edward. His face was white. They listened to the sound of the water with thumping hearts. The roar of the tide was doubled, trebled, multiplied over and over in their hard-walled cell. The reverberating echoes now filled up the intervals between the forward thrusts of the waves. Eleanor had to shout to be heard.

"Think of something! Quickly!"

But then they were lifted again. The shell was caught by the crest of the newest wave and cradled gently on it. Eleanor slid to one side, falling against Edward. She clutched him, and they rolled over together as the wave began to suck the shell backwards. It was caught up then by a new wave, higher than the first, and thrown violently forward and downward. For a terrible moment it was buffeted by the surf. Then they could feel it rolling over and over on firm sand once more. The waves fell away. But the next wave would be upon them very soon.

Eleanor lay limply where she had been thrown, moaning with nausea. Edward leaned up on one elbow and felt sorry for her. The tossing wasn't so hard for him. He had always liked roller-coasters and wild rides. But Eleanor got sick on an ordinary swing. "I wish she could get out of here," Eddy thought to himself, "even if I have to stay inside."

And it was this thought of Edward's that pushed its way out of the chamber, too big for even so stately a mansion. The door opened. Outside the sky was suddenly blue. For a moment Edward and Eleanor lay still, staring at the bright light of day. Then they scrambled to their feet and tumbled out the door. They were free, and standing once more on the scooped lip of the shell.

"Come on, quick!" shouted Eddy, yanking at his sister's arm. "Don't look back!"

One ghastly glimpse was enough for Eleanor. Waves as high as ten-story buildings were approaching, one behind the other, reaching down their foaming tops as if to look threateningly at them. "Run, run!" they screamed at each other. And they ran. They ran on the hard wet sand until they came to the end of it, and then they started struggling with the dry sand, where their feet sank in and the going was slow. But the water still pursued them. Frothing and boiling behind them, it stretched long watery fingers after them, filling up their footprints as fast as they made them, licking at their heels, a chest-high surge of tide rushing close after. Soon they were ankle-deep in water, and then the water foamed waist-high all around them.

"Hold hands and dig in," cried Edward. They leaned forward and hung on. Almost, almost they were pulled down and back by the thick sucking of the returning wave. But then at last it left them alone, and they were left high, but not dry, on the shore. They had barely enough strength to pull their feet from the mushy sand and stagger on again to safe ground in the high grassy dunes. There they lay down, gasping, with their faces to the sun, to rest.

They woke up exhausted.

"Oh, that was terrible," said Eleanor. They looked at each other with wan faces. Then they both looked across the room at the bookcase against the wall. The shell lay there on top of it, seeming very ordinary and very small. They got up and went across the room to look at it. Were the pearls still inside?

Eleanor swept aside her tangled hair and held the shell against her ear. But the sound of the sea made her shiver, and she took the shell away from her ear again. She held it in her hand and looked at it. She ran one finger over the spotted volutes at the center. Was her pink pearl still there?

"Shake it," said Edward. She did, and there was a sound, a tiny noise, the minutest hollow rattle.

"There *is* something inside," said Eddy. "Give it to me!" He shook it beside his ear. "It must be a pearl, still in there," he said. Then artfully, skillfully, gently, he tipped and maneuvered and shook the shell. It was like one of those games in which a little piece of BB shot rolls into a hole, if you tip the glass-covered box just right. The openings in the shell walls were still there, and Eddy managed to coax the object farther and farther from the central chamber toward the outside. Once he almost had it all the way out. Then Eleanor jostled his arm by mistake, and he could hear the thing rattle its way backwards through many a hard-won door. "Now see what you've done," he said angrily.

"I'm sorry," said Eleanor, looking bleakly at him. Delicately he worked it back again. Then at last, with masterful adroitness he brought it out of the last chamber. It rattled through the door and rolled swiftly out into the iridescent mouth of the shell.

It was a pearl. But it was a very, very small one. It was the seed pearl that Edward had pretended to play ball with. Ned and Nora must have found all the rest.

"Oh, where is my pink pearl?" said Eleanor, looking sadly at the infinitesimal bead in Edward's palm. "That would have been worth thousands of dollars! These little ones are a dime a dozen!"

20

"X" MARKS THE TREASURE

"WHERE IS UNCLE Freddy going?" said Edward, turning to gaze in surprise at his uncle, as he darted out past Edward through the front door, carrying a hammer and a suitcase.

It was snowing again, a wet vengeful April snow. Aunt Lily hallooed after Uncle Freddy and ran after him with his galoshes and umbrella. Then she came back and explained it to Eddy. "He has a notion to live in the yard, sort of camping out," she said uncomfortably.

"But we don't have a tent," said Edward.

"Oh, he's taken it into his head to live with Nature, like Thoreau. He's going to live in the old apple tree. It's hollow, you know, and he's going to board over the top and put on a door—"

Uncle Freddy galloped up the porch steps again, and ran past them, looking for a saw. "You three can settle down in the old chicken coop!" he babbled. "I've just been looking at it. It has the most delightful view!"

He was gone again. "You see," said Aunt Lily gloomily, "I finally told him about the house, and the back taxes, and how much we owe. First, he wanted us all to go straight to jail."

"To jail?" said Edward.

"Henry went to jail for not paying his poll tax, and Uncle Freddy would just love to go to jail because of taxes, too. Then I tried to explain to him that they wouldn't put us in jail anyway, for not paying, they'd just take the house away from us. Oh, Eddy dear," said Aunt Lily, "Mr. Preek has given us just two more weeks to pay all the back taxes. And I haven't even earned half the money! I thought perhaps we could borrow from the bank, but Mr. Preek is president of that, too, and of course, he said no. Well, I tried to tell all this to Fred, but he just got very excited. 'Who needs a house?' he said. 'Why should gay butterflies be entangled in a spider's web?' You know how he is." Aunt Lily leaned on the doorframe, rubbing her forehead.

"But why can't we live in the chicken coop?" said Edward. He thought that sounded like fun.

181

"Because Mr. Preek will take it all, house, land, apple tree, chicken coop, everything." Aunt Lily was close to tears. She went inside and shut the door. Edward went out to watch Uncle Freddy.

He found his uncle working busily around the hollow shell of the old apple tree. Edward helped him. Together they nailed up some old boards in the branches to form a sort of piazza that might have come from Never-Never Land. Then they slapped up a set of crazy steps, leading up to it. Wet snow plopped down on the earnest pair, but Uncle Freddy didn't seem to notice. He trotted back and forth to the cellar for a little potbellied stove, and soon he had it installed inside the hollow tree trunk, with a full scuttle beside it, and a jointed stovepipe carrying a cheerful column of smoke up and away from his board-roof. Another gorgeous discovery in the cellar was a colossal pumpkin, which provided something to sit on and completed the furnishings of the interior. Draughts were kept out with a gay checkered tablecloth gathered across a string, for a door. Then Eddy ran out of the house with an armload of torn sheets and discarded fringed bedspreads, and soon Uncle Freddy was frisking all over the tree, festooning it with awnings and draperies and playful canopies. His open umbrella was hung up to make a front porch for visitors to wait under, and as a final gallant touch Uncle Freddy ran up his striped muffler to the topmost branch.

They stood back and looked at it. "Who needs more to keep out the cold?" said Uncle Freddy proudly. "Whoops! I've forgotten to invite my friends!" He ran back into the house for Waldo and Henry, and soon he had set them up on orange crates that were wedged between branches. Before long their large noses and the tops of their heads carried dollops of wet snow, but they gazed straight ahead in their usual wise way, looking perfectly at home.

Uncle Freddy found a little branch of pine and nestled it around Emerson's shoulders. "Oh, Waldo dear," he said, "how right you are! Not the body, but the spirit must be the architect of gigantic structures! It must build itself a house, and beyond its house a world, and beyond its world a heaven! It must! It shall! Its dominion is as great as Caesar's!" He snatched up a piece of the torn sheeting and draped it over Eddy. Then he snapped a twig off the pine branch and wound it around his nephew's ears. "Emperor Edward!" said Uncle Freddy, chucking him under the chin and sweeping him a low bow, "in toga and laurel wreath! King of his own castle!"

Edward strutted pompously for a minute, dragging his sheet over the wet snow. Why couldn't they always just play at housekeeping with Uncle Freddy? Why did they have to be serious and anxious in a real house with Aunt Lily?

But he soon decided why. The snow suddenly turned to rain, and leaked through the cracks in the ceiling of the hollow tree. They squeezed themselves inside Uncle Freddy's narrow parlor and shared the pumpkin. But the stove hissed and steamed and smoked. It drove them choking out of doors and back to the big house—the big house that was their protection against wind and cold and rain and snow and sleet and frost and hot sun—a protection that would be theirs for only a little while! Then what would they do for a home? Eddy found Aunt Lily and pulled at her dress and asked her.

"Now don't you worry. I've got it all figured out," said Aunt Lily. She was doing her best to put a good face on things. "We'll just move to Boston and live in a flat." She was moving swiftly around the kitchen table with a handful of spoons, knives and forks, and banging them down in their places, hard. "We'll still be all together, and that's the important thing, whether we live in the poorhouse or a palace." She was reminded, then, of a song, and she began to sing it, sailing around the kitchen in rhythm and setting the plates down in graceful swoops to mark the ends of phrases. . . .

I dreamt that I dwelt in marble halls,
With vassals and serfs by my side!
And of all who assembled within those walls
That I was the hope and the pride!
I had riches too great to count; could boast
Of a high ancestral name;
But I also dreamt, which pleased me most,
That you loved me still the same!

"Oh, I'm sorry," said Eleanor, "let me!" Setting the table was her job, and there she was, sitting in the rocking chair with her wet shoes up on the radiator, reading a book! She jumped up and took the tray of dishes. How could she have been so lazy? Poor, wonderful Aunt Lily! She was working so hard, and against such odds, and yet she still sang cheerfully about marble halls!

"Marble halls?" Eleanor stopped suddenly, with a glass halfway to the table. There were marble halls in the treasure-poem written on the window!

A treasure made of ivory,
A palace for the soul.
Melodious marble halls
A treasure map enfold.

Melodious! The clue could be a song! This song! Could Prince Krishna have known it? Of course he could! Aunt Lily might have sung it to him, long ago! Eleanor could imagine it very well—Aunt Lily sitting at the piano with the big bow in her hair, singing the song about marble halls, with Prince Krishna looking shyly over her shoulder. But where was it, the printed sheet of music?

Eleanor hurried to finish setting the table, then she flew to the parlor and lifted up the top of the window seat. The inside was filled with books of music. Rummaging in it, Eleanor thought about the words of the song. How well they fitted, and how they must have struck home to Prince Krishna! For *he* must have lived once in marble halls, with vassals and serfs by his side, and of all who assembled within those walls, *he* must have been their hope and their pride! He had riches too great to count (undoubtedly) and he could boast of a high ancestral name (he was a prince, wasn't he?), but what would have pleased him most of all? If Aunt Lily had loved him still the same! It was perfect!

Eleanor found it then, at the bottom of the pile, a yellowed piece of sheet music, its edges crumbling with age. She turned back the cover to look at it, and a piece of paper slipped out of it and fell into her lap. She took it triumphantly to Edward, and together they studied it.

There was no doubt about it, it was a map. "And there's the 'X' where the treasure is," exulted Edward.

"It's not a map exactly," said Eleanor. "It's more like a plan, a house-plan. See? It's like a huge building with lots of rooms."

"What building could it be? Is it anything like our house?"

"No, our house doesn't have those curving side things sticking out. Could it be some other building in Concord?" They decided to look up and down the village streets after supper and try to find a building like it.

Up and down they tramped, in the freezing dusk, but without result. Except for their own, all the other houses were simple squares. Even the Town Hall was just a set of rectangles, and so were all the churches.

"We might as well never have found the map, for all the good it's doing us," said Edward irritably. "There never was such a building, at least nowhere we'll ever find." He was sitting in his pajamas on the edge of his bed.

It was disappointing! Eleanor crawled under the covers and lay on her side. She found herself staring nervously at the Jack-in-the-box in the corner. For the first time she wondered if it was really sensible for the two of them to go on sleeping in the tower room. The last dream had been so terrible! And they never seemed to come any closer to Ned and Nora, and the treasures hadn't been good for much, anyway, and most of them never even turned up at all. And there was that Jack-in-the-box. . . .

But the hook on Jack's box was tightly fastened. And Eddy had stuffed the mysterious plan with its spot marked "X" into his pajama pocket and pulled the covers up over his head. Eleanor looked at the dark diamond in the window and sighed. Was the game becoming too dangerous?

Well, tonight would be the last time. Tomorrow, she decided firmly, they would move their belongings downstairs, first thing.

21

THE PALACE FOR THE SOUL

I T WAS PITCH-DARK, but Edward could feel the wall, and he could sense that it towered very high.

"Are you there, Eddy?" It was Eleanor, whispering nervously. She twisted her fingers firmly into his pajama-top and walked close behind him. "Where do you suppose we are?"

Edward ran his hand up the wall. "Feel how big and square these stones are," he said, "maybe it's a fort."

Just then he stumbled over something large, and Eleanor collided with him. Eddy ran his hand to one end of it. It was long and cylindrical, and it felt like ribbed metal. "I know what it is," he said. "It's a flashlight. Where's the button to turn it on?"

He found the button, but then he couldn't budge it. When he tried to push it, the whole flashlight slid forward. Eleanor tried, but it slid out from under her, too.

"I know," said Eddy. "I'll sit in front of it with my back to it, and you push the button." That worked. Eddy leaned back with all his might, and Eleanor shoved on the sliding button with all *her* might. At last it gave, and Eddy's back was suddenly lit up. It was dark no longer. Together they turned the flashlight toward the wall.

"Look at that," said Eddy. "Why, there isn't anything holding those stones together at all! If we had bumped it, the whole wall could have fallen on us!"

Eleanor looked at the wall with her head on one side. The stones looked oddly familiar. She shifted the flashlight so that it shone this way and that. "Of course," she said. "We should have guessed. It's the block castle."

They were standing inside the gate, in the courtyard. Beyond stood the palace itself, with its arcaded walks running off to left and right. It was enchanting, the way the whole giant structure had kept the feeling of being a toy. The courtyard had a patterned floor made carefully of alternating red and white bricks. Platforms rose up from it, and everywhere there were stairs, rising up to the platforms, or sunk into the floor and leading to cozy-looking spaces with primitive-looking furnishings made out of the blocks themselves. There was about it all a sense of many levels—of many stepped, arched, tunnelled, columned shapes to play in. Eddy and Eleanor settled the flashlight so that it lighted up as much of the courtyard as possible, casting deep black shadows behind obstructions. Then they dodged happily about.

Eleanor was a ballet dancer. She soared and leaped among the drummed columns of the arcades, her nightgown billowing behind her and her hair flapping up and down. Her bare feet loved the feel of the smooth stones.

Edward was Trebor Nosnibor. He ran up and down the stair-steps pretending to duel with an enemy. He jumped from a top step to the tiled floor, with a marvelous thrust of his foil, right through the enemy's stomach! Aiyee!

Eleanor sailed through the air at him. "Look at me!" she cried.

"En garde!" said Edward.

Then all at once they stopped, and blinked at darkness. The flashlight had flickered and gone out for a fraction of a second.

"The battery!" cried Eleanor. "We're wasting the battery!" She ran to the flashlight and tried to turn it off. But it was a full minute before the two of them finally managed to pull the switch. Then they didn't know which way to go. They would have to turn it on again.

But first they sat in the dark and thought. Which way *should* they go? Suddenly Edward smote his forehead in the dark and felt in his pajama pocket for the treasure map. It was still there. Laboriously Eleanor helped him turn on the flashlight, and then Eddy held the plan in front of it. They studied it hastily.

"Of course," he said. "Why didn't we see it before? Here are the curving pieces on either side, those long porches you were running around in. And the 'X' is over there on the right side." They tried to memorize the plan. "Through the middle door, and along the hall, and then you're in a big room, and you take the door on the right, and then the second right, and that goes up the stairs where the arrow says 'UP.' The treasure must be up there near the top of that tower."

He lifted the front of the flashlight and directed it at the tower. "Look, quick," said Eleanor, catching at his arm. There were two people walking there, moving away from the tower. Their heads disappeared and reappeared as they moved along a row of windows. It was the lost children.

Edward was saddened by experience. "That's the last we'll see of them, I suppose," he said.

"Well, come on," said Eleanor. "They're probably looking for the treasure, too. Maybe we'll all find it."

They found their way to the middle door of the

block palace, then switched off the flashlight and groped their way along the narrow hall. The flashlight was a dreadful encumbrance. Once it jarred against the blocks, and there was a grating noise as one drum of a column slid sideways across another and shifted out of line. Eleanor and Edward froze, their hearts thumping. But the shifted drum continued to bear its load. They walked on, then, with the most extreme care, their cautioning whispers echoing in the low-vaulted space.

Then the echoes of their whispers changed. They had an emptier sound. Edward lifted up his head and tried to stare around in the darkness. "Whooooeeee!" he shouted.

"Whoooeee, eeee, eeee," came back the echo.

"We're in the big room!" said Eleanor. "It must be enormous!" She gazed blindly about. "Now, take the second right, then the first right."

"No, no," said Edward. "It was first right, then second right."

Eleanor was sure he was wrong. So once again they had to go through the difficult maneuver of turning on the flashlight in order to check the map. But the light expired almost instantly, going out in a momentary feeble glow from the filament, and leaving them in a darkness that seemed all the blacker for the certainty that they could no longer exchange it for light.

193

"But I *know* it's first right, second right," said Eddy stoutly.

"Who's the oldest?" said Eleanor snappishly. "I say it's second right, first right, and *I know!*"

There was an angry pause, then, while the two of them scowled into the darkness at each other. "Go ahead," said Eleanor. "*Be* wrong, if you want to. You go first right, and I'll go second."

"All right," said Eddy instantly. He started to walk away. Eleanor could hear his footsteps moving confidently along the right-hand wall. She felt suddenly engulfed by the darkness. "No, no, wait!" she cried, and ran to catch up with him. "All right," she said, grabbing his small warm hand in relief, "we'll go your way."

It was almost a pleasure to walk without the heavy flashlight. They soon found the opening that was the "first right" and turned into another corridor. Slowly they shuffled along it, brushing their hands along the right-hand wall. They walked for ages without finding the first opening.

"You see," said Eleanor peevishly, "I was right. Let's turn and go back."

"I found it!" said Eddy triumphantly. He was walking in front, and his fingers had suddenly swept off the monotonous surface that was the wall and stretched out into nothingness. "Here's the first right!"

From there it was only a little distance to the next opening. "This is it," said Edward, patting carefully in front of him, and feeling a rising set of steps. "We're at the base of the tower."

They climbed the steps, and were aware that it was getting lighter outside the palace walls. Through the chinks between the stones the blackness had turned from pitch-black to midnight-blue. Then they came out into the arcaded room at the top of the tower. On the other side was the opening to the passageway where they had seen Ned and Nora walking. And at the end of the passage was a lighted room.

Eddy pointed, and whispered excitedly. "That's where the treasure is," he said.

"Do you suppose the others are still there?" said Eleanor. Surely that would be too good to be true.

But they were. At the end of the passage and down a shallow set of steps was the treasure chamber. And in it were the lost children and the palace for the soul.

The treasure was an ivory carving of the Taj Mahal, the great tomb that had been built by an Indian king for his dead wife. Ned and Nora were looking at it, and walking around it and wondering at it. Nora was feeling the delicate filigree of the carving, and Ned was holding a candle and moving it to light up first one side of the building, then another.

They were so close, the lost children, Edward could almost touch them. He wanted to take their hands, and pull them back—back through castle and courtyard and wall and dream and all—back to the present time and the bright morning—back to Aunt Lily and Uncle Freddy. He hurried down the stairs and ran out into the room, calling to Ned and Nora. But they didn't seem to see him. He ran from one to the other. "Look," he said, "look at me! I'm Eddy, Edward Hall, and I've come for you! See me, see me? Look, here's Eleanor, too!"

But they didn't see. Gently, without seeming to avoid him, they began to move away. Walking slowly, looking back at the ivory palace, carrying the candle, they left the treasure room by a door in the opposite wall. Edward stared after them. Eleanor came down into the room and stood beside him and shook him. "They can't hear us," she said. "They had this dream long ago. We've come into their dream, but they can't come into ours."

Sadly they turned to look at the treasure. Its domes and towers shone palely in the strengthening light from outside. But then something happened. There was a distant terrible sound.

They turned their heads. Accompanying the sound was a vibration that made every block in the building tremble slightly against its neighbors. Eleanor and Edward shrank back against the wall and listened. The sound occurred again, and once more the building shook. What was it? It was a kind of frightful gathering, releasing, springing sound, of such violence that it was like the bouncing and crashing of a giant iron ball.

They ran out into the passage again, the floor shuddering beneath them. Then they stopped, and stared in horror out of one of the arched openings. The sound was made by the giant Jack. He had come loose from his box, and he was hurling himself forward by jumping up on his great spring, in gigantic leaps of crushing power. Now he coiled down upon himself, then he recoiled enormously upward and came down again in a nearer place with dreadful, crashing destruction. They saw him lurch against the distant wall, saw it topple, and saw him gather himself to spring again. The big face seemed half a mile away, and yet it seemed to be looking in at Edward. He grabbed Eleanor's arm, and started to run. But she pulled him back against the wall. "Someone's coming," she said.

Someone was running along the passageway. As they turned to look at him, the Jack-in-the-box made another battering, disastrous lunge at the outer wings of the block castle, and the blow made a shower of small bricks topple into the corridor. The bricks fell, one after another, against the running figure, but he seemed not to notice. He was calling out, with a low, urgent voice,

"Nora, Ned, where are you?"

It was Prince Krishna. He passed by them, very near, looking beside himself with concern, and disappeared around the corner into the room where the treasure was. Edward and Eleanor started to run for the stairway in the tower.

But then disaster struck. A great crack appeared in the floor, cutting them off. They stood hesitantly, looking out the window. With each spring the Jack-in-the-box had increased the momentum of his recoil, and now he made a towering extension of himself into the air above their heads, and came down like a sledge-hammer, with a wrecking, trampling force that destroyed the central front of the block castle. There was an avalanche of stone. Heavy slate-blue pieces from the roof toppled and fell with deafening thunder upon the supporting walls below, and these gave way and collapsed outward. Rapidly the whole palace shivered itself asunder, until it was once more just a disordered pile of blocks, toy blocks of assorted sizes and colors and shapes, hundreds and hundreds of them, all ready to be built up again into a pretty tower, or a bridge, or a lighthouse, or a "belvedere" or a "mausoleum," by some lucky boy or girl.

But Edward and Eleanor were not lucky. For them these toys were giant boulders, far heavier than themselves. Eleanor found herself clinging unhurt to a ledge at the top of a mountain of fallen stones. But under the mountain (which had become a "mausoleum" indeed) was a very small and fragile boy. The castle had collapsed upon Edward.

Eleanor woke up with a horrid start and a cry. She looked across at Edward's bed. Between them the block castle on the table was in ruins. Some of the pieces lay on the floor, some on Edward's bed. Edward lay still. Eleanor climbed out of bed and looked at him. His eyes were shut and his face was ashen. On his forehead was an immense black and purple lump. "Eddy!" whispered Eleanor. She shook him gently. She hissed his name. But he didn't wake up.

Then Eleanor ran for Aunt Lily. Aunt Lily gave little more than a quick look, and then she went downstairs hastily to call the doctor. When the doctor came he did his best for Edward. But it was hours before Eddy woke up. And when he did, it was only to talk feverishly, in his own strange Backwards English, and throw up with an ugly nausea, and drowse off again. Awkwardly and cautiously, Uncle Freddy and the doctor carried him downstairs to his own bedroom. His family hung by his bedside. Not till the next day could he hold anything down, or stay fully awake and know what was going on around him. The doctor said he had very nearly had a fractured skull. Eleanor knew the doctor thought she had thrown the blocks at Edward, and she felt miserable.

But Eddy was getting better. Several days later he was able to come downstairs for meals, pick at them feebly, and climb wanly back upstairs to bed. Not all the way upstairs, of course, to the tower room, but just to his own old bed in his own room on the second floor. Aunt Lily had forbidden them to sleep in the tower room, ever again. She had begun to have odd and uncomfortable feelings about that room.

"That's all right with me," Eleanor had said. Why, they were lucky Edward hadn't been killed! Terrible room, terrible dreams!

Not until Edward was really well and whole again did they even go back there to look for the treasure, the ivory carving of the Taj Mahal. Would it still be there, they wondered, buried and broken under the ruins?

The blocks were still there, strewn in disorder over the table. Eleanor began carefully removing some of the ones on the top of the pile. "The treasure room must have been about here," she said. She looked uneasily at the Jack-in-the-box, but he was shut up innocently, withdrawn from the scene of the crime.

"Look," said Eddy, "it isn't all broken. Some of it is

still standing, underneath." Swiftly he began lifting off blocks. Eleanor had a sudden thought, and stopped his hand.

"Do you know what it will mean if we find the treasure still there?" she said.

"No," said Edward, "what?"

"It will mean that Ned and Nora never woke up from that dream to find it themselves."

Edward looked at the blocks under his fingers. "That's right," he said. Then, one by one, he lifted them off, until he came to the long rectangular blocks that roofed the treasure room. Eleanor held her breath and bent over. Her red hair brushed the bandage on Edward's forehead, as he picked them up carefully and delicately and set them aside. They looked in. The little room was empty. Ned and Nora must have opened the castle up and taken the treasure out, and then put the blocks back together again.

Eleanor and Edward stood up together. Well, that was that. Eddy started to whistle. He bent down and picked up the big wooden box in which the blocks had originally come. He started to put them away in the box.

They would never know, now, what had happened to Ned and Nora and Prince Krishna. But Eleanor was glad it wasn't the same terrible thing that had so nearly happened to Eddy.

22

THE BUBBLE PIPE

I T WAS THE EIGHTEENTH of April. Next day would be
the historic nineteenth, Concord's great day. It was
on the nineteenth of April in 1775 that the battle had
taken place at the North Bridge, climaxing the chain of
events set into motion by Paul Revere, and beginning
the Revolutionary War. Tomorrow all the schools and
stores would be closed. There would be the usual
parade down the Milldam with everyone in uniforms of
one sort or another, ending up at the Bridge for a patri-
otic address by the Governor of Massachusetts.

It was to be an especially great day for Uncle
Freddy. He loved the parade. He looked forward to it all
year. He had his own Minuteman outfit and his own tri-

corn hat, and he would march, as always, between the Concord Independent Battery and the selectmen.

Today he had rummaged among his belongings for his tricorn hat and had set it at a cocky angle on his sandy hair. Now he was sitting out-of-doors in the April sunshine, in the doorway of his hollow tree, blowing bubbles. For a pipe he was using his own corncob, doing terrible soapy things to the insides and sending tobacco-stained bubbles up into the warm air.

For the cold had broken at last. The day was as warm as any day in June, and the apple tree had put on a brave show of buds on its few old branches. Edward and Eleanor were quite giddy with the warmth, after the long winter. Rashly they ran around with bare feet on grass that was newly green.

They were overjoyed with Uncle Freddy's bubbles. Eddy knew where there was another bubble pipe, and he ran all the way to the tower room to get it. It was the clay pipe that had belonged to Ned and Nora. Then he and Eleanor took turns with the pipe and Uncle Freddy's soap mixture.

The bubbles came easily. The soap mixture was just right. Bubbles bounced swiftly off the end of the clay pipe and surged gaily upward.

Uncle Freddy blew one high, high up into the apple tree. When it fell, it perched right in the middle of Ralph

Waldo Emerson's marble forehead, looking like a huge transparent boil, or a transcendental idea just bursting out of his noble brow.

"The crystal sphere of thought!" cried Uncle Freddy, standing up and waving his tricorn hat. Then the bubble popped, leaving a damp ring on Waldo's head like the mark of a wet glass.

Eleanor blew long chains of bubbles. She blew Siamese bubble twins, joined together. Then, miraculously, she blew a bubble inside a bubble. "Look, Eddy, quick, look!" she said. The two bubbles rose for a second, turning gently at different rates of speed, and then they fell swiftly. Then the inner one nudged the outer one and burst. The single larger bubble, lighter now, rose again. Uncle Freddy stood transfixed and watched it go. It wafted back and forth on invisible currents of air, soared as high as the roof, then disappeared over the southwest gable. Uncle Freddy's Adam's apple stuck out as he watched it with backthrown head.

"Oh, Waldo," he said, "did you see that? How like your remarks about circles!" He stretched up his arm and patted the stony necktie of his old friend. Then he started climbing the tree, to try and catch another glimpse of Eleanor's astonishing bubble.

"How like a man's life are concentric circles," he

ranted as he climbed. "He is imprisoned in the smallest till a new idea breaks him out of it and enlarges his horizon! But that horizon, too, may hem him in, until he bursts it, too, with a larger, bolder truth, and expands another orbit on the great deep!"

Uncle Freddy scrambled along one rotting limb, his eyes on the heavens, quoting Waldo—

> *Nature centres into balls,*
> *And her proud ephemerals,*
> *Fast to surface and outside,*
> *Scan the profile of the sphere. . . .*

"Look out, Uncle Freddy!" cried Eddy, who had looked up just too late. Uncle Freddy came to the end of the limb and plummeted, still quoting, out of the tree.

But his fall was broken. Just at that moment someone passed under the tree, on his way to the back door. It was Mr. Preek. He was bowled over by Uncle Freddy's descending form and laid out at full length on the grass. Uncle Freddy rolled off Mr. Preek's vest in perfect health, only slightly stabbed by the Phi Beta Kappa key on Mr. Preek's watch chain. Edward and Eleanor looked on, horror-struck. But Uncle Freddy went right on with his poem.

Knew they what that signified,
A new genesis were here!

he said, gallantly helping Mr. Preek to his feet.

Mr. Preek was outraged. He was so angry he could hardly speak. First he had been attacked by a madman, then he had been grossly insulted and called a new genesis. A new genesis! Why, his mother was a Saltonstall!

When Mr. Preek finally found his voice, it was to tell Uncle Freddy in no uncertain terms that he had come to forbid him to march in the parade tomorrow, and what was more, that he now had proof that Uncle Freddy was criminally and dangerously insane, as could be testified to by these witnesses (Eleanor and Edward dumbly shook their heads), and what was *more*, that the Halls' house was to be put up for auction the day after tomorrow, that was Friday, unless 575 dollars and 97 cents were paid on the dot, THE DOT!

Uncle Freddy looked pale. He studied the inside of his tricorn hat. "The dot," he said softly. He looked up again at Mr. Preek. "A dot is a very small circle indeed," he said. Then he withdrew shabbily into his hollow tree, and pulled the drawstring of his checkered door.

But Mr. Preek went on inside the big house, laid it on the line to Aunt Lily, made her thoroughly miserable, and then left, slamming the door and clapping on his hat. His Phi Beta Kappa key had drawn blood from Uncle Freddy, and his words had seared Aunt Lily's soul.

Edward never had any trouble going to sleep. It was just a matter of fixing your pillow so that one shoulder was under it, drawing your knees up to your folded fists, and shutting your eyes. But when twelve o'clock struck he woke up suddenly and found himself thinking uneasily about Uncle Freddy. Could Mr. Preek really take him away to some asylum? And poor Aunt Lily! If only he and Eleanor had been able to find some of the treasures in time to save her house for her! Then she could walk right up to Mr. Preek and scatter rubies and diamonds carelessly in front of him, the day after tomorrow on the dot, just as Mr. Preek had said! Edward closed his eyes again and imagined himself drawing a large dot on the end of Mr. Preek's nose. He pictured himself picking up a huge ruby and aiming it at the dot and letting fly.

Eddy's knees were drawn up to his fists, his shoulder was under the pillow, and this pretty thought was dissolving into a dream, when suddenly he sat up, pushed back the covers, and rolled his legs over the side of the bed.

It wasn't too late, *yet*. There were still two days, almost. And the verses were almost all solved. There was the treasure that was—

> *Too precious to be bought,*
> *As perfect and as fair as*
> *The crystal sphere of thought—*

and there was the treasure chest hidden by the eye of
the bird, and that was all. Why shouldn't he, alone, be
able to find them? Eleanor didn't have to take any
chances, and *he* wasn't afraid of the old Jack-in-the-box!

Silently Edward padded up the attic stairs and
looked at the ladder-steps. In the moonlight they looked
inviting, beckoning. Sturdily he climbed to the top,
solemnly he walked to Ned's bed, and steadfastly he lay
down and pulled up the covers. The moon shone in like
a bubble of snow, and the diamond shed a rainbow of
round moons across the floor. For a moment Edward's
red lashes fluttered open and shut. Then they closed
down for good on his freckled cheeks, and Eddy slept
again in the hidden, forbidden chamber, the room from
which Ned and Nora had disappeared, so finally, so
utterly and so completely, so long ago.

Downstairs, Eleanor lay tossing and turning. When the
clock struck one she sat up wearily, punched her pillow
into a different shape, shifted her doll Joanna, and sank
down again on her other side. Then she got up restlessly,
feeling cross-grained and grumpy, and stood looking out

the window, mumbling to herself. The moon looked to her like a stone-cold hard-boiled egg, or a hard white bubble, a kind of big white sphere. . . .

". . . as perfect and as fair as the crystal sphere of thought." What on earth was the treasure "too precious to be bought?" That was almost the very last of them! Why couldn't she try to find it herself? It was Eddy, not she, who had been hurt in the last dream, and come so near to being—of course *he* should not try it, ever again. But she could! Why not? And no one needed to know.

Eleanor found her way to the ladder-steps and climbed up into the tower room. She had a dreadful shock when she saw Eddy sleeping in Ned's bed. He wasn't supposed to be there! But then, of course, she wasn't supposed to be there either. Oh well, they might as well both be in trouble together. The room seemed filled with a sense of doom. Eleanor lay down and woefully pulled the covers up over her head, trying to shut the doom out, and closed her eyes.

23

THE CRYSTAL SPHERE

BUT THE DREAM was charming. Prince Krishna was there, looking gigantic, and blowing bubbles. Giant bubbles. Great shining, wobbling balloons of bubbles, big as houses, drifting and floating about in the moonlight.

Eddy was there before her. He ran ahead of Eleanor, laughing, and tried to stand under a big bubble as it fell. The bubble billowed and wallowed about him, and there he was, inside! Miraculously the filmy walls surrounded him, and lifted him up to float buoyantly to and fro. Eleanor found a bubble for herself, and she, too, had a ride.

It was delicious—softly, gently wafting from floor to

ceiling, bobbing against it with a yielding bounce, and drifting delightfully to the floor again! Eleanor's bubble grazed Eddy's and joined it. There was a flat wall of soapy film between them. Their bubbles swayed along together for a while, then came to rest on the floor. Both bubbles burst in a shower of suds, and Eleanor and Eddy ran to board other bubbles. Prince Krishna's dim, kindly face smiled far above them, and he blew foaming clouds of bubbles, big and small. Eleanor and Edward played among them, batting at them and blowing them, and pelting each other with them. Then they floated around in them again.

It wasn't until Eleanor was nodding along high above the floor in her sixth bubble that she noticed something strange. The wall of the bubble seemed less elastic and yielding than the others had been. She pushed her fist into it and found that it resisted her pressure, giving way only slightly. The film was hardening. Its perfect transparency was milking over, and an oily slick of rainbow color had appeared on the outside. The bubble drifted to the floor, and Eleanor punched her way out. It burst with a rubbery snap. She was immediately engulfed by another. Its walls, too, were thickening. It carried her off, and she beat her fists against it.

Where was Eddy? Eleanor looked around wildly through the distorting curved walls of her bubble. There he was, looking up doubtfully, as a bubble plopped around him. It bounded off the floor and sailed swiftly past. Eleanor kicked her way out of her bubble, which was a few inches above the floor, and dropped heavily and painfully on her side. Then she picked herself up and ran around looking for Edward's bubble.

Bubbles were beginning to collide with one another with some force and rebound away again with a hard noise like the clack of ricocheting billiard balls. Eleanor was knocked down by one, just as Eddy's bubble hit the floor again, and she missed her chance. His bubble shot away. The one that had knocked her down was bigger than most of the others, and just for a minute she thought she had been mistaken—wasn't this Eddy's bubble, and not the other one? There was someone in it. But then she saw that there were *two* white faces pressed against the curving wall. The surface was beginning to mist over, but she could still see them clearly.

It was Ned and Nora. They, too, had been captured by a bubble! Would they be able to get out of it? But she must help Eddy, first. His bubble was floating down again. Eleanor darted around under it, made a rush at it, and caught it. She kicked it in, and Eddy fell out. His prison shrank into nothingness with a horrid flabby report like a backfire. They picked themselves up and looked around.

The sound of the collisions had become higher in pitch. Now it was the shrill, deafening sound of glass crashing against glass, as the thickened walls hardened still further and crystallized. Eleanor and Edward were surrounded by smashing, splintering cannonballs. They ran.

And as they ran, Eleanor thought with a sinking heart how wrong they had been about Prince Krishna. It *was* he, after all, who had made the pretty dreams go bad! Hadn't she seen him, blowing the bubbles himself? She looked back at the source of the bubbles, the big white bubble pipe, and saw it through the rainbow walls of another colossal bubble, which was falling right over her. The bubble enveloped her with a loud pop, and carried her off. But for a moment Eleanor forgot to fight against it. She continued to look upward. Prince Krishna was not blowing the bubbles, not any more! There was another face there, a huge Jack-in-the-box face, dim and shadowy and distorted, but unmistakable!

And of course it couldn't be Prince Krishna, because he was down there on the floor, looking very small. Eleanor began to kick at the glassy wall. Prince Krishna was looking about helplessly, fending off a boiling, shattering barrage of bubbles. Eleanor kicked and thumped. She must get out and reach him. Then, to her despair, she saw him look up in surprise as a heavy bubble encased him and lifted him off the floor. She knelt against her curving bubble wall and craned her neck to look after him. She mustn't lose sight of him. This, this, she knew, was what had happened to him! This was how he had been caught, and Ned and Nora, too!

Prince Krishna's bubble shot up higher—it was milking over. Suddenly it collided with another, and the two collapsed into a single huge sphere. Swiftly the surface clouded, but for a second Eleanor could see Nora's white dress, and the larger shape that was Ned—they were there, too. Their bubbles had joined into one. Eleanor watched, drumming her fists against her own bubble wall, as the bubble imprisoning Prince Krishna and the lost children underwent a process of locking and sealing. One by one, other bubbles approached it and snapped around it, until there were bubbles within bubbles within bubbles, spheres within spheres. With each encompassing bubble the surface became more opaque, until the outer one at last was a sleek and shining silver globe.

Eleanor recognized it. How could she fail to, she knew it so well? It was the gazing globe, the gazing globe that had stood so quietly, all these years, reflecting the out-of-doors in their own front yard! The crystal sphere that was to have been a treasure had become a prison!

Eleanor sprang at the wall of her bubble, hurling the whole weight of her body against it. It burst with a boom like the sound of river ice splitting and cracking, and she was free, falling and falling out of her bubble and out of her dream, and waking up sore and unhappy in her own bed.

Instantly awake, she sat up with a terrible question. Where was Eddy? She twisted herself about to look at her brother's bed.

It was empty! Eddy was gone! Eleanor leaped up and ran downstairs, half-falling down the ladder-steps. The door of Eddy's bedroom was open. She ran inside. That bed, too, was empty. Her heart thumping and drumming, Eleanor scrambled all over the house, searching in the dark, and calling in a trembling whisper for her brother. But she knew well enough where Eddy was. He, too, had been caught in the dream—caught like the lost children, caught like Prince Krishna. The game had proved too dangerous, after all. Eddy was lost, the game was lost! Hoping against hope, Eleanor stumbled around once more in Eddy's room. She felt under his bed, and poked in his closet. Then the sight of his dresser top, with its orderly arrangement of match-boxes, pennies, and bottle caps brought her little brother so sharply before her mind that she burst into tears.

Blindly she ran out of the room and up the attic stairs. Tripping and stumbling, she made her way up the ladder and looked about the little room. It was empty. Eleanor ran to the window and stared up at the diamond. Their troubles never would have begun if they hadn't found the writing on the window. Eleanor banged at the glass with her fist and kicked it with her furry slipper. "It's your fault, your fault, you horrible window! Why did we ever have anything to do with you?"

She wasn't kicking hard enough to break the glass, but she jarred the metal frames that held the pieces of colored glass together, and all at once one of the pieces came loose and fell at Eleanor's feet.

It was the diamond. She reached down and picked it up. It was so big it half-filled the palm of her hand. It lay there glistening. It seemed filled with light, as though it had gathered into itself glints from all the dimly lighted surfaces in the room, and focused and magnified them within itself. And there was something on the back of it, something that had been fastened to the other side of the diamond, the out-of-doors side which they had never seen, except from far away down on the ground. It was a small metal hoop. It made the diamond look like a finger ring. Eleanor slipped it over the middle finger of her right hand and looked at it. Then she turned swiftly and stared at the disordered blankets of her bed.

There was only one thing to do. She must get back in the bubble dream. It was the only hope of finding and saving Eddy. And she might as well be caught in it herself, if she couldn't rescue him, for how could she face Aunt Lily and Uncle Freddy without him? It was all or nothing.

Grimly Eleanor lay down flat on her back and stared at the ceiling. Hurry, hurry. But how could she hurry into sleep? Relax, be calm. Eleanor wrenched herself around in the bed and lay on her side. How could she be calm? She found herself staring wide-eyed into the dark, and she shut her eyes fiercely. Then she found that she was playing a nervous tune, using her upper teeth against her lower teeth like fingers on piano keys, playing the same rapid phrase over and over—di-di-di-DEE, di-di-di-DEE. She stopped that, and tried stiffening out all over, and then relaxing, toe by toe and joint by joint.

How long was it before Eleanor at last went to sleep? Not as long as she thought. She was thoroughly exhausted, and by the time she had relaxed all her toes, one by one—and the arch of her left foot, and her right—and her ankles, left and right, slowly—and her left shin—and her right—very slowly—and her left knee—and—and—

—Eleanor was sound asleep again, and groping her way back into the dream.

*   *   *

But the dream had become a chaos. It was a nightmare of glassy balls, crashing and colliding with sharp, smiting, shuddering sounds. The metallic reverberating noise was frightful. Eleanor stood in her nightgown, looking about fearfully, with her arms over her head. She sprang to one side to avoid the recoil of two balls which smashed together just above her. Oh, where was Eddy's bubble?

She saw it, then, spinning by. Eddy was looking out at her and calling something. But she couldn't hear. And there beyond him was the great silver sphere that contained Prince Krishna and the two lost children. Watch out! Here came a giant bubble! It was going to descend all about her and close her in!

Eleanor reached out her hands to fend it off. Suddenly, as it touched her hand, it shattered into a thousand pieces. What had happened? Then she saw where her strength lay. It was in her ring. She held her right hand up again. The ring made it heavy, so she encircled her right wrist with her left hand, doubled her right hand into a first, ducked her head, and flailed about her with the great stone. There was a shattering, shivering, sundering noise, as though all the window glass and crystal dinner plates and goblets in the world were being exploded into fragments at one time. The noise went grinding and crashing on. Eleanor kept her eyes clenched shut and her chin down on her chest, and flung her arms around above her head, battering and slashing at the bubbles. At last the noise stopped, and she found herself tilting at nothing. Slowly she lifted her head and opened her eyes and brought her arms down.

The bubbles were gone. They had shattered, every last one of them, into soapy rings on the floor. And there was Eddy, standing next to her. Prince Krishna and Ned and Nora were gone. But there was someone else there. It was the Jack-in-the-box. They stood face to face with the enemy at last.

Eleanor and Edward turned together and looked at him. No longer was he only a face seen vaguely through the shimmering sides of a bubble, nor an apparition in a mirror, nor a resemblance traced in the clumsy features of a snowman or the sharp beak of a bird of prey. Nor was he even a grim toy, with a giant spring, in a box. He was a man. A man in a turban. He spoke to Eleanor. "Give me the diamond," he said.

Eleanor put her hands behind her back. She tried to speak, but couldn't. She shook her head.

Then the man made a swift motion at his side. He was holding something, now, something that glittered in a curving shaft three feet long. It was a long knife, or a kind of sword. "Give me the diamond," he said again.

Eleanor said nothing, but she gripped the hand that wore the diamond with her other hand behind her back and looked doubtfully at Edward. What should she do?

Eddy was looking at the sword. He wondered why he didn't feel more afraid. The live enemy was just as ugly as the Jack-in-the-box had been, but he was made of flesh and blood, and that meant that you could trip him and he would fall, you could hurt him and he would cry out in pain. Eddy felt a surprising surge of courage. He stepped behind Eleanor. "Evig ti ot em," he said.

"What?" said Eleanor, looking blankly at him.

"Em, em, evig ti ot em!" he said.

"Oh," said Eleanor. She looked back at the man and twisted her fingers nervously. The ring slipped off her finger and she passed it to Eddy behind her back. Eddy put it on.

Then the man who had been the Jack-in-the-box lifted his sword over his head threateningly and advanced a step toward Eleanor. But Eddy had a weapon, too. His jackknife was in his pocket. He took it out and snapped out the longest blade. Then he jumped jauntily in front of Eleanor in his bare feet and his wrinkled pajamas. Impudently he flourished his three-inch blade at the long and terrible sword. Tauntingly he stuck out the small hand that had the big diamond on it. "Try and get it," he said, hopping around on two feet at once, in what he thought was professional fencing style, "I double-dare you!"

But the man with the sword stood menacingly still. He had no need for subtle footwork or for graceful parries and lunges. He needed only main strength and a long arm. And those he had. He was a grown man. Eddy was only a boy, and small for his age at that. The man towered over him. Then he lifted his sword high over his head and held it there with the flat side down, and started to walk heavily toward Eddy.

Eleanor fell back, with her hands over her mouth. Why did her mind work so foolishly? At a time like this it was making a little joke. "Two jacks," it said, "jack-knife and Jack-in-the-box. And if Eddy loses the fight we'll have to have a funeral, and then there'll be another jack—a jack-in-the-pulpit!" Eleanor found herself laughing hysterically. Oh, oh, it wasn't funny at all!

Slash! Down came the terrible sword. But Eddy's clever bouncing hops took him out of the way just in time. He danced away, then pranced back, waving his miniature snickersnee. Trebor Nosnibor seemed to enjoy this kind of thing. Eddy felt strong and fit, nimble and quick. He could hop back and forth in this swash-buckling way forever, and dodge and parry with one hand tied behind his back!

Again the man used the flat side of his sword. But

this time he swung it from behind and brought it around his body in a whirling level arc. Again Eddy jumped back neatly, and the long blade whistled on around. It carried the man around with it, and for a moment, Eddy had the advantage. He dashed forward, meaning to get within working range for his little knife. But wet soapsuds on the floor betrayed him, and Eddy lost his balance and fell down.

Now the advantage was all the other way. Eddy had landed face down. He rolled over and lay on his back. Over him, looking miles high, was the man in the turban, and over his head the sword was lifted high. Eddy winced and stared at it. But the man just held it there. He spoke hoarsely, his chest heaving. "Now you will give it to me," he said.

"Go ahead, Eddy," cried Eleanor, running forward, "give it to him!" She grabbed at Eddy's finger and tried to pull the ring off. He snatched his hand away. Then the man in the turban dropped to his knees and knelt heavily on Eddy's chest. He pinned down Eddy's arms and snarled at Eleanor. "Take it off," he said. Eleanor gave him a frightened glance. She reached timidly for Eddy's hand and tried to pull the ring off his finger. It wouldn't come. She tugged at it with all her might. But she couldn't budge it. She looked up apologetically at the awful face that was so near to hers. "I'm sorry," she said, "I-I can't get it off."

The man in the turban became savage. He jumped up with a roar and dragged the two children to their feet. Then he snatched Eleanor and with dreadful strength he held her two arms behind her back with one hand and pointed his sword at her with the other. He shouted at Eddy, "Give me the diamond!" Eleanor struggled with him, kicking out with her feet and wrenching her captive arms from side to side. But he held her fast, and now he had the point of his long knife at her neck. She could feel it making a sharp dent in her throat.

For the first time Eddy was frightened. He forgot to be Trebor Nosnibor, he forgot to be a fencing expert. It was all very well to shout double-dares, but what should he do now?

The man in the turban was holding Eleanor up off the floor by her pigtail. It hurt her like anything, but at least she had her hands free again. She used them to beat and scratch at the arm that was holding her, and she lashed out at the same time with her legs.

Hesitantly, Eddy held the blade of his jackknife over his shoulder in throwing position. If only Eleanor would stop wiggling, then he could aim. He shouted at her, "Eleanor, hold still!"

Eleanor heard him, and went limp. In an instant she changed from a kicking, scratching, clawing animal into a dead weight. The man was caught off guard. He fell forward, entangled in his own long sword and Eleanor's sprawling legs. Eleanor sat down on the floor with a heavy bump. There was a harsh cry.

Eddy saw his chance. The advantage was his again. His enemy lay on the floor. Now was the time to finish him off. He adjusted his blade between two of his fingers in the grip that gave him the surest aim, the one that sent the knife to the mark every time, point down. But he didn't throw it. Something stopped him. He waited for the man to turn over and get to his feet, so that the odds would be fairer. But the man didn't move. Eleanor sat on the floor where she had fallen, staring at him. Eddy waited. After a while he moved closer and bent over. Then he stood up and folded up his jackknife. "It's all right," he said, his voice shaking a little. "He fell on his sword."

Eleanor put the end of her pigtail up to her eyes and wept into it. She woke up sobbing.

But she stopped crying instantly, and got up. She walked across in the dark to Eddy's bed and reached out carefully to the place where his pillow was. Was Eddy's head there, where it should be?

"Ouch," said Eddy, "you've got your finger in my eye." He sat up and shook his head.

Eleanor hugged him hard. She had really, truly brought him back! Eddy pushed her away.

"Listen," he said, "what's that?"

The clock was striking four, but there was another sound. It was a knocking at the front door.

24

THE LOST ARE FOUND

*T*HE KNOCKING WAS far away, but it was distinct and clear. Edward and Eleanor started downstairs, but Aunt Lily was ahead of them. She swept down the upstairs hall before them, tying the ribbons of her dressing gown, her hair hanging loosely to her waist. Down the stairs she went, past Percival and Mrs. Truth. Eddy and Eleanor hung back and peered down the stairs. Who could it be?

Aunt Lily turned on the porch light and reached for the handle of the front door. Then she stopped, and put her hand on her heart. Through the glass she could see three figures standing outside, waiting for her to open the door. Then, with shaking hands, she opened it slowly and stood back.

There was a tall man standing there, wearing a turban on his head. Beside him stood another man, almost as tall. His hair was dark red. And there was a woman in a white dress, with hair that was reddish gold. The tall man in the turban stepped inside. He was looking at Aunt Lily with tears in his eyes. "Lily," he said brokenly, "you are more beautiful than ever."

But Aunt Lily was twisting her hands in the front of her dressing gown. "Where were you?" she said. "Oh, tell me where on earth you have been, the three of you!"

"We were prisoners," said the man in the turban, "but now we are free, and we've come back home again." Then he put his arms around Aunt Lily and kissed her.

"Oh, Lily!" said the woman in the white dress. And she kissed Aunt Lily, too. So did the tall man with red hair.

Eddy and Eleanor looked between the bars of the stair-railing, and wondered. The tall man was Prince Krishna! But where were Ned and Nora? And who were these two strangers? But now Aunt Lily was calling them in a trembling voice to come downstairs and meet their "Aunt Nora" and their "Uncle Ned."

Aunt Nora! Uncle Ned! How terrible! Eleanor and Edward looked at each other in dismay. Then they went downstairs and shook hands politely. Why weren't Ned and Nora children like themselves? But of course, they had been children when they were lost, and that was long ago. Of course they would have grown up, in all this time. Eddy stared up at his good-looking, friendly new uncle and tried not to mind. And Eleanor was kissed by her beautiful aunt with the golden-red hair, and she, too, tried to forget the little *St. Nicholas* girl in the picture.

Then Uncle Freddy, aroused by the noise, shuffled downstairs. He was struck all of a heap, and wept, pulling a bandanna handkerchief out of his bathrobe pocket. He kissed everybody again, and Prince Krishna embraced him with a new look of pain on his face, and tenderness. Eleanor realized that of course he hadn't "known" about Uncle Freddy until now.

Then Prince Krishna turned to the stairway. He looked up at the face of Mrs. Truth. "I think we need a little more light," he said.

Eddy started to tell him about the wiring, and the burned-out bulb, but then he stopped. The light was on! Prince Krishna had turned the switch, and Mrs. Truth's star was shining once again, flooding the big dark hall with incandescent light.

Prince Krishna smiled up at Mrs. Truth. Then he started to run up the stairs. He bounded up them, taking three at a time. Where was he going? Edward and

Eleanor ran after him.

Uncle Ned took Aunt Lily's hand. "It's all right," he said.

Prince Krishna seemed to know just where he was going and how to get there. He walked swiftly along the balcony to the attic door. Then he ran up those stairs, too, with Edward and Eleanor at his heels. He climbed right up the ladder-steps and stood up in the small tower room, looking very tall. The children scrambled up behind him. There was just enough dawn-light coming through the clear glass pane of the keyhole window so that they could see. They looked around fearfully. Would there be something lying on the floor, something dark and terrible?

But there was nothing there. Prince Krishna was looking for something else. He strode across the room to the Jack-in-the-box.

"Oh, look," said Eleanor softly. The Jack-in-the-box was greatly changed. The lid was open, and the spring was drooping over the edge of the box. The head lolled on the floor. Prince Krishna lifted it a little way with his foot, and let it fall. It flopped on the floor and lay still. There was no strength left in it. The spring had sprung. Picking it up in his hands, Prince Krishna dropped it down inside the box, and it lay there in a state of limp collapse. Gently, then, he let the lid fall. There was no need even to hook it. The Jack-in-the-box was nothing now but a child's plaything, and a broken one, at that.

Then Prince Krishna straightened up and turned to the children. And he was so magnificent in his black coat and his turban with its peacock feather, his eyes were so wise and his look so simple and kind that Eleanor felt quite overcome. He was older, too, she could see that now. There were wrinkles beside his eyes and thoughtful lines across his forehead.

"Is this your room?" he said, looking at Edward.

"Yes," said Edward shyly, "mine and Eleanor's."

Prince Krishna smiled at Eleanor. He kissed her cheek. Then he shook Eddy's hand. "I am very glad to meet you," he said.

Then they went downstairs. Uncle Freddy had brought Waldo and Henry in from out-of-doors and set them up in their old places beside the hearth, and now the reunion was complete. The family party walked through the velvet curtain and stood together in the faded splendor of the parlor. Aunt Lily, looking radiant and hardly older than Eleanor, made everyone sit down. Then Prince Krishna started to talk. His voice was low and intense. And as he talked, all the years melted away— the years during which Aunt Lily had wondered, the years during which she had yearned over the lost children and Prince Krishna—as she began to understand

230

what had happened to them.

"We were imprisoned by my uncle," said Prince Krishna.

"Your uncle?" said Aunt Lily.

"His name was Jacaranda. He was my father's brother."

Jacaranda! The name was unfamiliar, but the sound of it brought before Eleanor and Edward the vision of a face, the face of the man in the dream who had fallen on his sword.

Prince Krishna's story began with a letter that had come to him one day, in that time long ago when he had been a guest in Aunt Lily's house. It was a letter from his uncle, and the envelope was edged in black. It bore the tragic news that Prince Krishna's father was dead. Then the letter went on with a proposal. Prince Jacaranda begged Krishna to give up his right of succession, to step aside in favor of himself as the next Maharajah, and to give up to him the state treasures that were in his possession.

Prince Krishna had been grief-stricken. He had answered the letter at great length, pouring out his grief. And he had confessed to his uncle his sorrow at leaving behind the new friends for whom he had come to have so much affection, and his dread of the grandeur and ceremony that would accompany his new duties. He had described to Prince Jacaranda his happiness in the good and simple life he had found in Concord, his joy in his new-found friend, his love for Lily, his fondness for the children, his pleasure in the games they had played together. He reminded his uncle that he, too, as a child, had played the same games, the old games that were traditional in the family of the Maharajah. But he had told him that in spite of his sorrow he would return to India, and take up the burden himself. He had refused Prince Jacaranda's request.

"But what for?" said Eddy.

"Because my uncle was an evil man," said Prince Krishna. "I knew how terribly my countrymen would suffer from his greed and tyranny. I could not sacrifice their good for my own."

"What did he do then?" said Eleanor.

Prince Krishna glanced at Ned and Nora. They were sitting soberly beside him, listening. His face looked haggard. "He did something very strange. He sent a present to the children."

"It was the Jack-in-the-box!"

Prince Krishna nodded gravely. "The Jack-in-the-box, indeed," he said. "It became his viceroy, his representative, a villainous copy of him in plaster and wood and coiled wire. And he used it to capture the children." Prince Krishna's voice betrayed his anguish. "It was my fault," he said bitterly. "If they had not befriended me, it would never have happened. But we had become very fond of one another, and they were my friends, my young companions. To amuse them I played with them the kind of games I had known myself as a child. And the children were very clever. I had to make the games harder and harder. At last I invented one that was hardest of all. And they were eager to begin. Innocently they set out on it alone. One by one they sought and found the baubles I had hidden for them. But in my ignorance I did not know how dearly they were bought with danger! My pleasant little trails had become nightmare journeys, fatal and terrible! Trusting me, the children did not complain. Instead they went on and on, until they were trapped, kidnapped, lost! Only then did I become aware of what was happening, only then when the children were gone. And then my uncle wrote to me again." Prince Krishna sank his head into his hands.

"He threatened me," he said. "If I would agree to his demands, he would release the children. Otherwise I, too, would be imprisoned. Sick at heart, I wrote to him, and put him off, day after day. Desperately I tried to find them and rescue them myself. I entered myself upon the game we had played, following the trails, and discovering at every turn the dreadful shapes my patterns had taken. And at last my attempts failed. My uncle fulfilled his threat, and I, too, was caught and imprisoned."

Prince Krishna straightened up and looked at Aunt Lily. "But now it is all over, at last," he said. His smile went around the room to include Edward and Eleanor, and they felt a rush of devotion to this new and remarkable friend.

"But what was it like?" said Aunt Lily, with a gesture of concern. "Where were you imprisoned? In India? Why didn't he kill you? And, oh, Nora dear, how did you all endure it? We've missed you so!"

Nora looked at her gravely. "We weren't uncomfortable at all," she said. "And we think that someone has been helping us for a long time."

"Yes," said Ned, "one by one the doors that shut us in have been unlocked, until there was only one door left, and tonight that one, too, was broken open. And here we are."

Aunt Lily was bewildered. "But who set you free?" she said.

Prince Krishna looked at Eleanor. She blushed. Then he turned slowly and looked at Edward. Edward turned red, too, and grinned. Prince Krishna smiled broadly at them. "Whoever they were," he said, "they were true friends, and very gallant ones indeed."

Eleanor felt glad. She couldn't look at Prince Krishna, she was too shy. So she looked instead at the peacock feather on his hat. And the peacock feather seemed to be looking back at her. There was an eye in the middle of it, a blue eye, with a pupil of dark iridescent green, and there was a dash of yellow like a highlight across the green—

> *Eye of bird, eye of fowl,*
> *Hides the treasure chest—*

Why, a peacock had more than two eyes! He had dozens—in his tail!

25

THE TREASURE CHEST

*E*LEANOR STOOD UP. She left the room, unnoticed, and brushed through the curtain that hung in the parlor arch. Standing in the light of Mrs. Truth's lamp she looked up at the stair landing. Percival was there as usual, looking a little dazzled and frowzy in the unaccustomed brightness. Eleanor walked slowly up the stairs, picked him up in her arms, and brought him into the parlor. She set him up in the middle of the room, and everyone stopped talking and looked at him.

"Dear old Percival," said Nora. She got up from the sofa and went to him and stroked his dusty feathers. Eleanor looked at the "eyes" in Percival's straggling tail. Surely there was nothing under them that could be a treasure chest? They stuck out sparsely and stiffly into thin air. But there was another "eye" on Percival's back, oddly out of place. Why had she never noticed it before? She pointed to it.

"That's where you put the treasures when you found them, isn't it?" she said.

"Treasures?" said Nora. "Oh, yes, I'd forgotten. Are they still there?"

Then Edward understood, too, and he clapped his hands and crowded in close to see. Prince Krishna stood up and watched them silently, his arms folded across his coat. Eleanor lifted the feather that looked like an eye. Under it there was a little piece of green ribbon. She pulled at it, and a piece of Percival's dorsal section slid back, revealing an opening as big as her two fists. Within was the sheen of a piece of white silk, a great roll of it, filling the space inside.

Eleanor and Edward lifted the roll of silk out carefully and laid it on the table. It was knobby with lumps. Slowly they unrolled it. And one by one the missing treasures were revealed.

The first was the ruby brooch. Against the white silk it looked as brilliantly red as a Valentine. It was just like the ruby in Eleanor's dream about the snowflake wedding dress. Then there were nests of pearls, dozens of them, scores of them, hundreds of them, big as marbles!

Eleanor found her favorite pink one and rolled it in her hand.

After the pearls came the most valuable treasures of all, the diamonds that had been stars. They kept trickling and tumbling out of the silk, from fold after fold, masses and clumps of them, to lie glittering in heaps on the table.

And in the very center of the silk, where it had been swathed in layer after layer of protecting folds, was the delicate filigree carving in ivory, the miniature Taj Mahal. It was as white as the white pearls, with four minarets and a shining central dome. "How beautiful!" said Aunt Lily.

Then Eddy remembered something else. He was still wearing the big glass ring from the window. It was turned around on his finger so that the stone was cupped inside his hand. He twisted it off and laid it on the silk beside the ruby brooch.

Prince Krishna came forward and reached out his hand. He picked up the window-stone and held it up to the light, so that it sparkled and glowed with color.

"That's *our* diamond," said Eddy proudly.

"Of course it's not real," said Eleanor. "It's just the glass lump from the window."

Prince Krishna took Aunt Lily's left hand in his. Gently he slipped the ring on her fourth finger. "Thank you," whispered Aunt Lily. She held her hand up to look at the ring. "For glass it is very beautifully cut," she said. Her voice faltered.

Prince Krishna smiled at her. "It is the Star of India," he said simply.

"The Star of—of—" stammered Aunt Lily.

"But that's a real diamond, isn't it?" said Eddy.

"Yes," said Prince Krishna. "It was the crown jewel my uncle wanted most."

"But why didn't he just take it?" said Eddy. "It was right there in the window!"

"I expect he tried," said Prince Krishna. "But he must have known it was impossible. The Star of India cannot be taken. It can only be given."

Eleanor was dazzled. The Star of India! It had been in their own house all this time, right in the room where they had slept so long! Prince Krishna must have used it to scratch the mystic verse on the glass, and then he must have broken out the central piece of the window and fastened the ring in its place. And the Star of India could not be taken! That was why the man in the dream, the man who was Krishna's uncle, hadn't tried to tear it from her finger, or from Eddy's—that was why he had had to keep asking for it. He had hoped to threaten them into giving it to him freely. And that was why she hadn't been able to force it from Eddy's finger—

Then, with a shock of surprise, Eleanor realized that it had been given to her. It was true that she had asked for its help in a rude enough way, but she had not taken it—she had been given it. It had been theirs for the asking all along.

Uncle Freddy was dazzled, too. He teetered back and forth in his rocking chair, and then he jumped up and began to stride excitedly up and down. The others were bent over the table, examining the jewels. All but Aunt Lily—she looked up at Uncle Freddy and worried about him. She knew how badly the loss of the children had damaged his mind—would the shock of their restoration damage it still further? She laid a gently restraining hand upon his arm. But Uncle Freddy brushed past her and went on pacing back and forth, his chin sunk into his chest, his hands behind his back. It was true—something was happening to Uncle Freddy's addled brain. Into that clouded pool of ancient quotations a new spring was rising—and disturbing and roiling the waters. Uncle Freddy tossed back his head in his agitation, and then stopped. What was that? Had he heard something?

"Boooooom—boooooom—boooooom!" Why, it was cannons! It was the cannons at the Old North Bridge announcing the dawn of April nineteenth, Concord's great day! Uncle Freddy laughed out loud. It was like remembering, suddenly, that it's your birthday. He ran to the window and threw up the sash. He quoted Paul Revere at the top of his lungs. "The British are coming!" he shouted. Then he dropped to one knee, held up an imaginary musket and squinted along the invisible barrel. Everyone looked up and stared at him. Uncle Freddy quoted again, this time from Major Buttrick, commander of the Minutemen at the bridge—"Fire!" shouted Uncle Freddy, "for God's sake, fire!"

And Eleanor did. She didn't mean to. It had occurred to her all at once that the bust of Louisa May Alcott had been left out of the family celebration entirely and was missing all the excitement. Henry and Waldo had been invited, and even Percival was there—but poor Louisa had been left out in the cold! So she ran out into the hall and came back again, dragging Louisa on her tall stand. But then the cannons boomed, and Uncle Freddy shouted, and Eleanor was so startled that she tripped over the worn carpet and lost her hold. The unfortunate Louisa toppled from her stand, took Uncle Freddy on the side of the head and smashed into smithereens on the floor.

Uncle Freddy dropped like a stone. Eleanor was beside herself with remorse. "Oh, Uncle Freddy!" she sobbed, "Uncle Freddy!"

But the blow was only a glancing one. It didn't hurt

him badly, and to everyone's surprise and joy it had a very lucky and wonderful effect. It was just enough of a stunning shock to finish a process that had already been begun.

When Uncle Freddy woke up again he was leaning back in Prince Krishna's arms, blanketed in an old afghan from the sofa. He looked around the room with eyes that were marvelously clear. No longer was he poor daft Uncle Freddy—once again he was Professor Frederick T. Hall, with all the dignity and wisdom that that name had once implied. His good sense had been completely restored. His mind was as sharp as a knife, as deep as a well, and as sound in wit as it had ever been—and that was very sharp and very deep and very witty indeed. Eleanor and Edward, leaning over him anxiously, saw once again the uncle they had seen in the dream, the one who had left footprints in the sand. They looked at him in awe.

The new Uncle Fred shook his head and sat up. He looked at the broken remnants of Louisa and chuckled. "I never liked her anyway," he said.

Aunt Lily fell upon his neck and burst out crying. "Oh, Fred!" she said, "it's you! You've come back to us, too, at last!"

26

THE AIR OF FREEDOM

S O UNCLE FRED MARCHED IN the parade after all. His
tricorn hat hid the bump on his head, and his step
was strong and confident. Mr. Preek marched
ahead of him with the rest of the selectmen, and now
and then he turned himself halfway around and looked
back doubtfully. But he didn't try to throw him out. The
change in Uncle Fred was apparent for all to see.

And everyone did see it. When the parade had come
to a halt at the Battleground, and when the horseman
had thundered up in imitation of the historic ride, and
when the Governor of Massachusetts had given a
speech, and when the Commander of the American
Legion had given a speech, and when the guns had

sounded again, there was a general outcry. Some of the older citizens of Concord had heard Frederick Hall give orations in his youth, and now they called for him again. They lifted him up on the platform bodily, and cried, "Speech! Speech!"

So Uncle Fred gave a speech. He stood on the platform and smiled around at everyone, and then he started talking easily about Concord's air. He said that it was the air of freedom itself, and that it had first started blowing about Concord's streets and fields long ago, in the dying breaths of the men who fell on that April day in 1775. He said that it was the same air that Thoreau and Emerson had breathed, and that it had expanded their minds, too, with the buoyant gas of liberty. . . .

"My friends," said Uncle Fred, "that air still gently blows in Concord, in inspiring zephyrs, in ecstatic gusts—inhale it, citizens of Concord! Breathe deep the ether of Concord's illustrious past! Then, with inflated breasts, look to the rainbow arch that sparkles anew in Concord's skies, brightening yet once again her wondrous air! Exhale the past! Inhale the future! Let your lungs, too, become a bellows of truth! Breathe it forth once more, and fan with it Concord's ancient flame, until she shine before the world yet once again, in new glory!"

He stopped, then, and stepped modestly down. Uncle Fred had stopped quoting. He was on his own at last.

But his audience wouldn't let him go. They pushed him back up and made him take bow after bow, while they shouted and whistled and clapped. Several people had been so overcome by gasping obediently for deep breaths that they had lost consciousness altogether by over-breathing, and they had to have their heads inserted in paper bags to restore their wits. One of these was Miss Prawn. She awoke to remember that she herself, Madeline Prawn, had had the honor to sign the asylum-commitment papers for this divine man, and she fainted away again, overcome with pride.

At home again after the parade, Edward and Eleanor were ready for bed at last. They were worn out. They dragged themselves up the front porch steps.

"Wait," said Eleanor, "I forgot to look." She went down the steps again and stumbled around the forsythia bushes that were spraying their yellow blooms across the grass. There it was, the cement pillar of the gazing globe in the front yard. But there was nothing on it at all. Around it lay the shattered pieces of the big silver globe, like shiny pieces of broken eggshells. Eleanor picked up one of the pieces and looked at it. The bubble had really burst, the crystal sphere that had been a prison had been broken open, and the prisoners set free at last. Another battle had been fought in Concord on April nineteenth, and like the first battle, it had been fought and won.

Eleanor yawned. Eddy rumpled his hair with his hand and rubbed his eyes—and together they went upstairs to bed.

27

THE BOUNTIES OF SPRING

*T*HE MORE SHE THOUGHT about it, afterwards, the stranger it seemed to Eleanor. There was Concord, on the one hand, sober and real and historic and American, with its memories of the Minutemen and Emerson and Thoreau and Louisa May Alcott, and its stores on the Milldam, and its dignified houses on Main Street, under the elms. All that was familiar and everyday. But there on the other hand was the Mysterious East! And Prince Krishna, and the Star of India, and the pearls and diamonds that were a Maharajah's treasure trove! What an outlandish mixture! Which was which? Where did one begin and the other end? Then suddenly Eleanor saw what blended them together. It was the house she lived in, her own wonderful house. There it sat, with its fantastic domes and oriental-looking towers, right there on Walden Street, harboring inside it an old-fashioned New England transcendentalist as ardent as any that had ever lived in Concord. Nothing could be surprising that happened within its walls. It was a special place, as unique and wonderful as the home of Emerson, or the Old North Bridge, as worth preserving as Orchard House or Walden Pond or even the birthplace of a President of the United States. Eleanor thought of Mr. Preek, and worried. No one must burn it down!

She needn't have been afraid. On Friday morning one of the smaller diamonds was sold, and the back taxes were paid to Mr. Preek right on the dot. He harrumphed and complained and tried to make objections, but there was nothing he could do. The money was all there, including the interest, and Aunt Lily's house was saved. And there was enough money left over to put it in apple-pie order for the wedding.

Mr. LaRue was to repair the house and paint it. He came one day with a hammer and a hundred-pound keg of eight-penny nails, and went to work on it, tapping loose shingles back into line, replacing broken clapboards and slats, and firming it all up once more. Then he brought over twenty-five gallons of white paint and started to slap it on. It took a long time. Edward helped him out, after school. He painted the railing of the front porch, dripping white splashes all over the bushes underneath.

Everyone was busy. Ned was encamped in the Concord Library, preparing for the entrance examinations for Harvard College. Prince Krishna and Uncle Fred were hard at work, collaborating on a new book. Prince Krishna was hurrying to finish his share as fast as he could, because he had received some remarkable news. He had written to India to say that he was alive and well and was coming back. But then there had been an urgent cablegram in reply, a long message that described the mysterious death of his uncle, the reigning Maharajah, and begged him to return at once. His countrymen, said the message, awaited his arrival with relief and joy. Prince Krishna thought about it, and talked it over with Fred, and worked on the book. They sat all day at a table in the parlor, writing it, and reading paragraphs aloud to each other.

And all over the rest of the house the three women-folk were turning things upside-down, spring-cleaning. The dust flew. Nora swept, Aunt Lily scrubbed, and Eleanor polished Mrs. Truth with brass polish. Aunt Lily looked around, when they were all done. She stopped in the front hall. Mrs. Truth shone dull gold, and her star shone brightly on the new stair carpet. "Let's have the wedding right here," said Aunt Lily.

But Eleanor had another marriage to arrange, first. Among the wedding gifts which poured in upon Aunt Lily and Prince Krishna there was one from the trustees of the Concord Library. It was a replacement for the bust of Louisa! The library had long possessed its twin, and one day the trustees got together, took it down from its pedestal, and pulled it in a little wagon to the house on Walden Street.

Eleanor opened the front door, took one look and clapped her hands. Uncle Fred was there, too. He slapped his hand to his forehead and said, "Oh, no!" But then he laughed. No longer did he forbid the match, and Eleanor lost no time in beginning again her monumental romance. Louisa's reincarnation looked just like new. It wasn't chipped at all. Henry proposed immediately, Louisa accepted graciously. Waldo united them, of course, and Uncle Fred himself ruefully gave the bride away.

The other wedding, the flesh-and-blood wedding, was perfectly lovely. Aunt Lily was beautiful in the snowflake wedding dress. She descended the staircase carrying a bouquet of appleblossoms from Uncle Freddy's tree. Prince Krishna stood below, looking up adoringly at his bride. Mrs. Truth's star shone, and Aunt

Lily's choir sang wedding music in the background. For a minute Timothy Shaw's heart felt like breaking, but then he saw Nora, coming down the stairs behind the bride. She was wearing rose velvet and carrying white lilacs, and Timothy felt much better. (He went daringly up, instead of down, at the end of the song and brought out a soaring note that made Nora smile down into her flowers.)

Eleanor wore a new pink dress, with the big pink pearl around her neck on a chain. Edward was ring bearer. He carried the Star of India on a pillow, his face expressing suffering nobly borne. (Trebor Nosnibor wouldn't be caught dead in a blue serge suit!) Uncle Fred gave away his second bride in the course of a week, and Ned was the best man. Percival lent the wedding an air of pomp and glittering splendor, and Waldo, Henry and Louisa looked on, giving the couple their venerable blessing.

The wedding breakfast was held out-of-doors. It was a fine fair breezy day in May. Aunt Lily and Prince Krishna sat at the head of the table, with Aunt Lily's veil billowing out behind her in the warm wind. Uncle Fred stood up and proposed a toast. "To the bride and groom!" he said.

Everyone sipped his champagne, while Uncle Fred recited scraps of a poem by Emerson—

Wreaths for the May! for happy Spring
To-day shall all her dowry bring . . .
Knowing well to celebrate
With song and hue and star and state,
With tender light and youthful cheer,
The spousals of the new-born year!

"The spousals!" said Uncle Ned. "Hear, hear!"

"Now, Edward," said Uncle Fred, "if you'll just be the butler and pass around some more champagne, you'll fit right into the next verse." Eddy tugged obediently at the cork of a champagne bottle. It came out with a pop and flooded a burst of bubbling champagne all over his blue serge suit. Delighted, he licked some off his sleeve and passed the bottle while Uncle Fred went on with the poem—

Thou butler sweet . . . send the nectar round;
The feet that slid so long on sleet
Are glad to feel the ground.
Fill and saturate each kind
With good according to its mind . . .
And soft perfection of its plan—
Willow and violet, maiden and man!

Eleanor looked wistfully at Aunt Lily. "When will you come back again from India?" she said.

Prince Krishna smiled at her. "We just have to arrange for free elections," he said, "and sell the rest of the jewels to start some public schools. Then we'll come right home again."

"Aunt Nora and Uncle Fred are going to take good care of you while I'm away," said Aunt Lily comfortingly.

Nora squeezed Eleanor's hand. "Of course we are," she said.

Timothy Shaw was sitting next to Nora. He looked at her earnestly. "If there's ever anything I can do to help," he said, "don't hesitate to call on me, and I'll come right over. Any time at all."

"Aunt Lily," said Eddy, "what are you going to do with the Star of India? You're not going to sell that, too?"

"We're going to give it away," said Aunt Lily.

"You are?" said Eddy, in surprise. "Who to?"

"To an old temple I know of," said Prince Krishna, "an old temple that is very holy, where it will be safe forever." He looked around the table and smiled. "I'm afraid our pockets will be empty when we get back to Concord again."

Aunt Lily laughed. "We'll have to live in the chicken coop after all!"

"Now, Lily," said Uncle Fred, "I have a plan. I'll finish up the new book in no time, and then, you know what I want to do? Start a school! Right here in this house! Krishna can teach in it, too, when he gets back!"

"I would be proud to," said Prince Krishna. "What will our school be called?"

"Oh," said Uncle Fred modestly, "I thought we might call it something straightforward and simple, like 'Concord College of Transcendentalist Knowledge.' I'll get Mr. LaRue to make a big sign and put it up over the front porch."

Eddy stopped with a piece of wedding cake halfway to his mouth and figured it out. It was the best Backwards English he had ever heard. He whispered it under his breath. Then he gulped down his cake and ran around the back yard shouting it. Eleanor took up the cry. It was almost like a football cheer—

DROCNOC! EGELLOC! FO TSILATNEDNEC-
SNART! EGDELWONK! EGDELWONK! RAH!
RAH! RAH!

Benjamin Parks had been invited to the wedding, and he had a ball in his pocket. He jumped up, now, and tossed it to Eddy. Eddy caught it, and ran with it tucked under one arm. He had completely forgotten the wedding. He was Trebor Nosnibor, football hero. The game was tied, and there were only ten seconds left to play. "EGDELWONK! EGDELWONK! RAH! RAH! RAH!" shouted Eleanor, jumping up and down, and just in time, at the last possible second Eddy made a flying touchdown for Concord College in the vegetable garden, getting green stains all over the knees of his blue serge suit and grinding dirt into the wet front of his coat.

The coffee came in paper cups. Uncle Fred stood up again and banged on the table with the sugar bowl. He had forgotten, there was more of Emerson's poem about spring and the air of May—

> *Spring is strong and virtuous,*
> *Broad-sowing, cheerful, plenteous . . .*
> *So deep and large her bounties are,*
> *That one broad, long midsummer day*
> *Shall to the planet overpay*
> *The ravage of a year of war. . . .*
> *And where it comes this courier fleet*
> *Fans in all hearts expectance sweet,*
> *As if to-morrow should redeem*
> *The vanished rose of evening's dream!*

He sat down again, amid applause. The wedding breakfast was over. And Aunt Lily and Prince Krishna and Ned and Nora and Eleanor and Edward and Uncle Fred walked off together to the railroad station. The bride and groom were going away. They were all going away, really, into the mirror again, pulling shut behind them the doors of yesterday, and choosing among tomorrow's doors the right ones, the good ones. . . .